To my grandniece, Allison Danielle Anthony
With Jah love
Always stay clear of Trouble's barrel
— V. H.

For Bob & Patricia MacLachlan
— B. M.

THE ALL

JAHDU STORYBOOK

By Virginia Hamilton

Illustrations by Barry Moser

HARCOURT BRACE JOVANOVICH, PUBLISHERS

San Diego   New York   London

Library of Congress Cataloging-in-Publication Data
Hamilton, Virginia.
The all Jahdu storybook/by Virginia Hamilton:
illustrated by Barry Moser.
p.   cm.
Summary: A collection of old and new adventures
of Jahdu, the trickster.
ISBN 0-15-239498-2
[1. Magic — Fiction.]   I. Moser, Barry, ill.   II. Title.
PZ7.H1828A1   1991
[Fic] — dc20   90-47847

First edition   A B C D E

CONTENTS

The All Jahdu Storybook

*Now begins the time of
the magic trickster, Jahdu.*

JAHDU MAGIC

ONE LONG TI

ME AGO, THERE WAS JAHDU.

He was born in an old oven beside two loaves of baking bread. One loaf baked brown, and the other baked black. Jahdu didn't bake at all. But since that time, black and brown have been his favorite colors. The smell of baking bread is the sweetest smell to Jahdu.

The hot dust from the oven settled into him and became his Jahdu dust, like no other dust in the world.

Jahdu liked always to be running along. He was two feet tall. Yes, he was. And now, he'd been in the world one year. He made his home in the only black gum tree in a forest high atop the Mountain of Paths. Animal children also lived in the forest. From his tree, Jahdu could see them as they walked along the paths down to the valley and up again.

Jahdu thought the paths the animal children walked along were good and safe. And only these good and safe paths would Jahdu run along. But Jahdu was only a year in the world. He didn't know everything. No, he didn't.

One day, he was running along behind some animal children. All at once, the little animals stopped still.

Bandicoot Rat fell to the ground. He grew stiff and cried for his mother.

Bear Cub stood up on one hind leg. He hopped in circles, bumping into White-Tailed Fawn and stepping on Baby Otter. Bear Cub sang a wordless song.

Woodchuck, Raccoon Girl, and Wolf Child wandered away into the piny woods and were lost. Other little animals sat down on the path. They moaned and trembled all over.

It took Jahdu an hour to gather all the animals on the path again. He tied a rope around them and led them to a good, safe place. There, he let them loose.

I'd better get back to that first path, Jahdu thought. I'd better find out what could cause little animals to stop, hop around, and fall down.

Jahdu hurried to the first path. And something there he couldn't see tried to catch him. Jahdu was quicker than whatever it was, and he kept on running along. He stayed right on the path. Yes, he did. All at once, he fell into a hole full of thorns.

"Ouch!" cried Jahdu. "Thorns have points to hurt me!" He jumped out of the hole and bounced into a soft bed of sweet-smelling leaves.

"Woogily!" said Jahdu. "This funny path has good and bad about it. It can't be safe for little animals to walk along."

Jahdu kept to the good-and-bad path full of thorns and sweet-smelling leaves. He ran on and on until he came to a stream. He plopped down in it to cool himself.

Suddenly, thirteen crawfish started pinching Jahdu.

"Woogily!" Jahdu shouted, and he leaped out of the water. "This fresh stream has crawfish that can pinch the paws of little animals. I'd better find out where this funny path ends."

He hurried along the good-and-bad path full of thorns and sweet-smelling leaves and a stream across it with thirteen crawfish.

All at once, Jahdu ran smack into a banyan tree at the end of the path. He bounced off it and around it. Yes, he did.

"Woogily! How in the world did a banyan tree get into these piny woods on the Mountain of Paths? Running into banyan trees does not feel good," said Jahdu. "Little animals will hurt themselves if they go walking into banyan trees!"

Two animals lay up in the banyan tree, watching Jahdu.

"Oh!" cried Jahdu. One animal had a round, sweet face and a bell on its head. The other animal had a square, mean face and no bell anywhere.

"I've never seen anything like you," Jahdu told them. "What in the world are you called?"

"I'm Sweetdream," said the one with a bell on its head. It had a soft, kind voice.

"I'm Nightmare," said the other one in a harsh voice. "You're Jahdu, and we don't like you."

"For goodness sake!" Jahdu said. "Like me or not, I'm here to stay. Please tell me why there's a banyan tree at the end of a path where little animals walk."

"Because it's here," mean Nightmare said, "just as Sweetdream and I are here, and the path is here. We all go together, so there!"

Said Sweetdream, "My head-bell tinkles when little animals are walking along here."

"Then we use our charms to get them," grinning Nightmare explained. "It's fun watching our spells work on them."

"How do your spells work on them?" Jahdu asked.

Sweetdream spoke first. "My spell makes little animals stop, hop, and sing sweet songs."

"My spell makes them stiff," said Nightmare. "They fall down and cry. They moan and tremble. My spell makes them do bad things, too."

"Little animals ought to be able to walk along and do as they wish," said Jahdu. "It's not nice to use spells on them."

"We do as we please," said Sweetdream, sweetly.

"Nothing you can do will stop us," said Nightmare. "You'd just better be on your way."

Jahdu ran to the banyan tree and kicked it as hard as he could. "Come down from there, you awful things!" he hollered. "Come down, and I'll surely take care of you!" He kicked and he shook the tree until both animals up there turned a sickly color all over.

"Stop! You're making us dizzy!" yelled Sweetdream and Nightmare.

"We can't come down," Sweetdream said. "We're attached to this banyan. We can't ever come down."

Sure enough, the two animals grew like figs on the banyan's branches.

"Woogily!" whispered Jahdu. "Now I've caught you for sure!"

He ran around the banyan tree as fast as he could from happiness. The tree-grown animals couldn't get away from him. But he ran so fast, his Jahdu dust shook right out of him. Yes, it did.

Jahdu dust rose up into the banyan tree. It settled on Sweetdream and Nightmare. And they fell fast asleep.

Jahdu stopped running. "Did I do that?" he asked himself. "Woogily! Did my dust put Sweetdream and Nightmare to sleep?"

Wherever the Jahdu dust fell, it put things to sleep. Man Spider on the tree trunk got dust in his eyes and fell asleep. Big Blue Jay flying low near the tree got a whiff of Jahdu dust. She landed, asleep on her feet.

"Woog—i—leee!" shouted Jahdu. "I've got magic! I can put things to sleep! Maybe I have more magic. Let me see."

Jahdu wished there was no good-and-bad path, no Sweetdream and Nightmare, and no banyan tree. But nothing happened; nothing changed.

He had another idea. Jahdu ran around the banyan tree slower and slower and ever so slowly.

The Jahdu dust rose off the two animals growing on the tree. It rose off Man Spider, off Big Blue Jay, and off everything. Jahdu dust fell back into Jahdu. All that had been asleep woke up.

"I can wake things up," said Jahdu. "I've got another magic!"

Sweetdream and Nightmare yawned and looked around. "You shouldn't have put us to sleep," said Nightmare. "We do our work on the animals in the daytime so we can watch the fun."

"Not anymore," said Jahdu. "I'm going to make you do your work at night. Nightmare, you will have to sleep from daylight to nightfall. You'll work your spell at night and only on sleeping animals. And if ever you use your spell when it's daylight, I'll put you to sleep for a year!"

Nightmare looked sick and stayed quiet.

"Sweetdream can work her spell in the daytime only on little animals who sleep by day," Jahdu said. "But only once in a long while. The rest of your work you'll have to do at night on sleeping animals, the same as Nightmare."

Sweetdream smiled sweetly but said not a word.

"Never again will you have fun watching spells work," said Jahdu. "I'll get rid of the good-and-bad path. I'll put it to sleep for the rest of time!"

Jahdu ran very fast and put the path to sleep with his dust. Seeds of forest plants once under a spell began growing. He stood a moment where now pine saplings grew in a row. It was where the path once had begun.

He shouted down the path at Sweetdream and Nightmare: "No little animals will come along here. As you send your spells out on the night air, never again will they be strong. For the night air so light will carry only some of your charms."

So it was that Jahdu found his power. He had magic that could wake things up and put things to sleep.

"Woogily!" Jahdu shouted. And he went right on Jahduing along.

JAHDU was running along southward through a hot, empty land. "Woogily!" he whispered. "There's not much to look at to make the time go faster."

A strong wind blew in Jahdu's face. He heard a swishing sound on the wind. Then he saw a family of tumbleweeds coming toward him, heading north.

"Hey there! What's the big hurry? Wait up a minute," Jahdu called as the tumbleweeds passed him by. He turned around and followed them. But the wind helped the tumbleweeds more than it did him. "No way to catch *that* tumbleweed family," he said to himself.

"You're a long way from home, Jahdu," one tumbleweed hollered back.

"Well, I like to be always running along," Jahdu called after it. "But what's your hurry?"

"We're the last to leave here," yelled the tumbleweed. "We hope to reach the north mountains before nightfall."

"You were lucky to catch such a swift wind," called Jahdu. "If you wait just a minute, I'll travel along with you. I'm pretty much tired of this hot, empty land."

"We can't wait for you," all the tumbleweeds yelled back. "But do follow us north. For southward lies Trouble."

"Trouble?" said Jahdu. He stopped running. "Hey, tumbleweeds," Jahdu called. "What is it you said?"

The tumbleweeds hollered from far away. "Follow us, Jahdu. For southward lies Trouble . . . lies Trouble . . ." And the tumbleweeds were gone to the north.

"Woogily!" said Jahdu. "Those tumbleweeds surely were in a hurry. Wonder what sort of thing is Trouble? I'd better go southward and see."

So Jahdu went hurrying along. He ran and he ran southward through the long, empty land. He saw a few tall trees, but not one sound did he hear beyond the pa-lippidy-lippidy sound he made running.

"Woogily!" Jahdu said again. "I see some mountains southward. The tumbleweed family should have followed *me*. I like mountains better than empty land."

Closer to the mountains, Jahdu ran as quietly as he could. For they were not like any mountains he'd seen. When he was quite close to them, the mountains moved. Yes, they did.

With a sound like creaking, the mountains sat up. They stared hard at Jahdu.

"Woogily!" Jahdu came to a stop. "What in the world kind of sitting mountains are *you?*" he asked.

The mountains shook all over. They rumbled like thunder and made Jahdu tremble. "I'm no mountains, friend. I'm the giant called Trouble. Come closer, little friend, so Trouble can see what you're made of."

"Oh no, thank you," said Jahdu. "I'm really just passing through. I've known all kinds of mountains and a number of tumbleweeds," he added, "but I've never known anything called the giant Trouble."

"Well, now you do," said Trouble in a voice like drums. "And what might you be called, little friend?"

"You mean to say you've not heard of Jahdu?" asked Jahdu.

"Never in my life," said the giant Trouble.

"Everyone knows me," Jahdu told Trouble. "I'm Jahdu who is always running along. I just turned three feet tall. I live in a gum tree when I'm at home. And I have magic that I keep to myself."

Trouble laughed. "You come too close to Trouble, Jahdu," said the giant. "I think I'll just keep you from running along."

The great right hand of Trouble swooped down. Yes, it did. But already Jahdu had started running away. Jahdu ran, and he ran. The great right hand of Trouble just missed him.

The great left hand of Trouble swooped down. Jahdu managed to slip through its fingers. Trouble laughed in a thunderous roar. He stretched himself out along the southward landscape and propped himself up on his elbow.

Jahdu stayed out of Trouble's reach. He could see the giant was no kind of mountain. Trouble was bigger than fifty-two mountains.

The giant was clothed in gray. His eyes were rain-cloud dark, and his face looked as angry as a storm.

Trouble's teeth flash like lightning, thought Jahdu. And what a large earring he wears on his right ear.

"What are you staring at, Jahdu?" asked the giant. "You like my ears? Oh, it's my earring you stare at. Come closer, Jahdu, and I'll show it to you."

"Oh no, thank you," Jahdu said. "I really have to be running on."

But he went right on peering at the giant. Trouble's feet were as big as ships on the ocean. His legs were as long as highways.

There was a gold loop bright as the moon through Trouble's earlobe. A blue barrel hung from the gold loop. The barrel was as large as a standpipe. Screams and cries came from inside it.

"What in the world are those sounds from your earring?" asked Jahdu.

"Jahdu, those are my friends you're hearing," said the giant. "I like all my friends so much, I keep them with me!" Trouble laughed like thunder.

"I can tell by their screams and cries that your friends are in a barrel of Trouble!" Jahdu said. "I'm sure they want you to let them out, too."

"Screams and cries are sounds I like best," the giant said. "Besides, no one I put in my barrel ever gets out again."

"What sort of friends would even a giant treat so badly?" asked Jahdu.

"I don't care if they are good, bad, big, or little," said the giant. "I treat every kind of folks just the same. You see, I never bother them, but they always find me and swarm over me like flies."

"Woogily!" said Jahdu. "I surely wouldn't want to end up like a fly in your barrel!"

"Oh, come now," said Trouble. "Have a look. I've got a whole bunch of fine folks traveling with me."

With one huge finger, Trouble tipped his barrel so Jahdu could see inside. Jahdu climbed the tallest tree he could find to have a look. What he saw wasn't pretty. "That's about the worst sight I've ever seen," he said.

Jahdu saw birds in the barrel; they were so sad they covered their heads with their wings. He saw animals. King Lion was crying! He saw mothers and fathers and babies all huddled in a heap for safety. Jahdu saw just about every kind of folks in that barrel of Trouble.

It made him angry. Yes, it did. Jahdu looked fierce. "I don't like Trouble at all!" he said.

At once, Jahdu thought of a plan to free all those caught in Trouble's barrel.

He climbed down the tree and started running along close to the giant.

"You must set them loose," Jahdu told Trouble. "If you don't put that barrel on the ground and let everyone out, I'll have to free them myself!"

"Come ahead, little Jahdu," said the giant. "Come right on." Trouble's hand swooped down in a rush of wind and scooped him up.

"Oh, please, giant Trouble, don't put me in your barrel," Jahdu begged. "I was really just running along." He pretended to be frightened.

"You won't run along ever again," said Trouble. And—plop! He dropped Jahdu into his barrel.

"It's Jahdu!" shouted everybody in the barrel. "Trouble has caught Jahdu! It's the end of us for sure!"

"Hal-loo!" called Jahdu. "I want all of you to gather around me, please. We're getting out of here!"

"We are?" everybody asked.

"Of course," said Jahdu. "Do you think I would have let Trouble catch me if I hadn't planned to get free again?"

"Jahdu, you're wonderful!" everybody shouted.

Jahdu felt so proud, he said, "Woogily!" Yes, he did. Then he told everybody what they must do.

"Mothers and fathers, dig into the walls of this barrel. Babies, you scratch at the sides. Birds, peck with your beaks. Donkeys, you kick. You, King Lion, stop crying and use your claws to tear at the floors. We have to make lots of holes in this barrel. Cows, horses, set up a mooing and neighing. King Lion, roar, please, so Trouble won't know what's going on."

Everybody did as Jahdu said. But they never made a dent in Trouble's barrel. No, they didn't.

"Woogily!" Jahdu whispered. "I see I must outsmart the giant if I'm to free everybody."

While all the folks did their jobs, Jahdu ran inside the barrel. He ran faster and faster. Yes, he did. Soon, his dust rose up in the barrel and settled on everybody. One by one, everybody in the barrel fell fast asleep. Jahdu lay down and pretended to be asleep, too.

After a while, Trouble couldn't hear one scream or cry like music to his ears.

"Hey, friends," he said, "sing a little louder. I can't hear you."

Not one sound came from the barrel. Trouble took off the earring and peered inside. There he saw everybody lying on the bottom.

"Why, they've all fainted from the heat, even little Jahdu," said the giant.

Carefully, Trouble gathered everybody and Jahdu in his hand and lifted them northward. He put them down by a mountain lake. "I'll give my friends a chance to cool themselves," he said. "Then they will feel more like screaming and crying later."

24   Again, the giant stretched out across the southward landscape. At once, Jahdu got up. He ran around slower and slower and ever so slowly. Jahdu dust rose off everybody and settled back into Jahdu. Everybody woke up. Yes, they did.

"I outsmarted Trouble," Jahdu told everybody. "He still lies southward, resting. So be quiet, and hear what I say.

"Those who live in water, dive deep underwater and stay hidden," Jahdu said. "Those who like holes, go hide in holes. Everybody else, follow King Lion, for he knows where to find the oldest mountain cave. Trouble is sure to come searching for all of us soon. So hurry!"

It wasn't long before Trouble looked across the hot, empty land for his friends. He saw only Jahdu, who was running along just out of reach of Trouble's long arms.

"Little Jahdu," Trouble said, "that's the first time anybody's ever tricked me."

"I used my head and my magic," said Jahdu. "I outsmarted you, is all. There's no need for you to search for your friends, either. You might find one or two of them, but you'll never find everybody."

The giant shook with laughter. "I don't need to go looking for them, little friend," he said to Jahdu. "I've never had to go looking for anybody. For it's the truth that everybody comes looking for Trouble, and they always will."

"Not *me!*" said Jahdu. "I'll not come looking for you ever again!"

"Oh, sure you will," Trouble said. "You won't be able to help yourself. So, good-bye, little friend, until the next time."

Trouble turned away. With three giant steps, he was out of sight beyond the hot, empty land.

"Woogily!" whispered Jahdu. "I hope I don't run into Trouble again."
Jahdu didn't. No, he didn't — not for a long, long time.

Jahdu Outwits Young Owl

JAHDU had been running along over most of the earth. Sometimes he stopped awhile. But never did he stay long in one place. Wherever Jahdu stopped, he had to outsmart somebody. And anybody who had been tricked by Jahdu wouldn't let him get close enough to do it again.

One day, Jahdu was running in a wood with trees growing close together. The wood was warm and wet; vines grew as thick and round as large snakes. When the ground grew soggy, Jahdu swung along on the vines.

Jahdu had a bell-shaped pink cage tied to him by a piece of rope. He'd taken the cage just for fun, which wasn't nice of him.

The pretty cage had six parakeets in it. The owner shouted, "Bring back my parakeets, Jahdu!"

Jahdu opened the cage and let the parakeets fly away. The owner shook his fist at Jahdu. Jahdu laughed and kept on running.

He ran through the trees in the warm and damp place. Besides carrying the cage, Jahdu balanced a can of blue paint on his head. There was a small paintbrush sticking out of the paint. He had taken the paint from a farmer's wife. She'd been painting a gray chair blue. When she wasn't looking, Jahdu took her blue paint and put a can of white paint in its place. He'd taken the white paint from a fellow painting windowsills.

Jahdu stayed around long enough to see the farmer's wife pick up the now-white paintbrush. The chair turned white as she painted; she screamed and jumped away.

Jahdu laughed at the farmer's wife. Yes, he did. He went on running along through the woods, with the parakeet cage tied to him and the can of blue paint balanced on his head.

He happened to be vine-swinging along when he heard a sound of moaning and groaning.

"*Ooooh. Hoooo,*" the sound went.

"Woogily!" said Jahdu. "What in the world kind of sound is that?" He stopped his swinging and sat in a tree to listen.

"*Ooooh. Hoooo,*" the sound went again. It came from the tree across from Jahdu. Jahdu could make out a hole high in the tree.

"That is awful moaning and groaning. I bet an owl is in that hole up there," Jahdu told himself. "Owls are the worst moaners and groaners in the world. Think I'll stop up there awhile and have me some fun."

Jahdu placed the parakeet cage in his tree for safekeeping. He climbed down, putting the can of blue paint on the ground behind the tree. Then he went over there to the tree with the hole up high.

"Hey, up there," Jahdu called. "Who is it I hear moaning and groaning worse than anyone?"

There was silence high up in the tree. But then the moaning and groaning started again. Jahdu climbed up the tree and peered in the hole. "Just as I thought," he said. A small screech owl leaned against the wall of its nest. It moaned and groaned and held the feather tufts on its head.

"What in the world is the matter with you?" Jahdu asked.

The owl opened his eyes and rolled them from side to side. "It's raining, isn't it?" asked the owl. "It's pouring rain. It's been raining for days, hasn't it? My headache will never go away!"

"Oh, my goodness," Jahdu said. "It's not raining at all. The sun is blazing, and there's not a cloud for miles."

"Who are you?" asked the screech owl. He blinked his wide eyes at Jahdu.

Jahdu didn't want to tell the owl his name. No, he didn't. If the owl had heard of Jahdu, he'd surely fly away.

"I'm a friend come to help you," Jahdu said, kindly. "What is your name?"

"I'm Young Owl," said the owl. "My friend is Lilly Owl who lives at the edge of the woods. It's her birthday. I can't find a present for her, and that's why I have a headache."

"Well, give her a weasel," Jahdu said. He knew owls were fond of weasels.

"Lilly already has some," Young Owl said. "But she doesn't have a safe place to keep them."

Woogily! thought Jahdu. I know how to catch me an owl!

"Young Owl, I can help you," Jahdu said. "Just step outside, and I'll show you a fine gift for your Lilly."

"*Ooooh. Hoooo.* No," said Young Owl, holding his tufts. "My head-ache! The sun will make it worse."

"Well, close your eyes, and I'll lead you," Jahdu told him. "The present I have for your Lilly is in the tree across from here. Come along now."

The owl let Jahdu lead him by his wing over to the tree where the parakeet cage waited. He kept his eyes shut tight. Yes, he did. "I hope you know what you're doing, friend," Young Owl said to Jahdu. "I've *never* walked up a tree."

"Don't worry, a few more steps and we'll be up in the leaves. Then you may open your eyes in the shade," Jahdu said.

Soon, Jahdu and Young Owl were up in the branches. Sunlight fell brightly through the leaves. Just then, Young Owl came to the place right in front of the parakeet cage.

"You can stop now," Jahdu said. He reached around the owl to open the cage.

"Young Owl, open your eyes!" said Jahdu.

Young Owl opened his eyes. He saw the parakeet cage and gave out a screech. Yes, he did. Jahdu pushed Young Owl inside the cage and slammed the door.

"Woogily-wowl! Jahdu's caught a Young Owl!" Jahdu shouted.

"Jahdu!" Young Owl screeched. "I've heard about you, playing tricks for fun. Oh, please, let me go. I hate sunlight. I hate cages!"

"No, indeed," said Jahdu. "I'm going to sit here and sing you happy songs until I'm too tired to sing. I know forty happy songs, and I never grow tired of singing!"

Jahdu sat himself down. He had no one else to stop along with, so he had plenty of time. He sang at the top of his voice for the whole sun-filled day. Yes, he did.

Young Owl lay on the floor of the cage. He moaned and groaned. *"Ooooh! Hoooo!"* he cried. "I hate sunlight and cages! I hate happy songs!"

At the end of the day, Jahdu jumped down from the tree. "Well, Young Owl," he called, "I have to be running along. I'm sure your Lilly will come as soon as it's dark. She'll want a present, of course, so give her your cage."

"Ooooh. Hoooo," Young Owl moaned.

Jahdu picked up the can of blue paint and put it atop his head. Young Owl watched him.

"Would you mind telling me why you have that can on your head?" Young Owl asked.

"Because I intend to paint somebody blue!" Jahdu said.

Jahdu went on his way with the paint can atop his head. Every now and then he swung along on the vines as big as snakes. He had a good time swinging and running along. He hadn't found anybody he felt like painting blue. But he knew he would find somebody sometime. Yes, he did.

So that is how Jahdu tricked Young Owl. He had tricked almost everybody by now. And almost everybody had grown very, very tired of Jahdu.

JAHDU was running along and telling everybody to get out of his way. Everybody always did get out of Jahdu's way. But this time, somebody wouldn't. And that somebody was Grass.

Grass lay on the ground in one dull shade of gray as far as the eye could see. Jahdu shouted at him. "Get out of the way, Grass, for Jahdu is coming through."

Grass didn't move at all. No, he didn't. Jahdu lay down on Grass and stretched out as far as he could.

"How do you like that, Uncle No-Color?" Jahdu said to Grass. "Jahdu is heavy, isn't he?"

Grass didn't say a word. But he couldn't feel the sunlight with Jahdu all over him, and he grew cold. When Jahdu called him Uncle No-Color, he became angry.

Grass lifted all his young gray blades straight as arrows. He pushed them against Jahdu with all his might. And the strain on his young gray blades turned each and every one of them green! It happened a long time ago, but to this day you can tell Grass whenever you chance to see him. For each and every one of his blades is still green.

Well, Jahdu laughed. He got up slowly. He yawned two or three times and gave no more thought to Grass, who had turned green. He ran and he ran until he came to dry, hot sand.

"Woogily!" Jahdu whispered. "This sand is hotter than anything I know that is hot."

Jahdu saw Ocean lying as calm as could be on the horizon where the hot sand ended.

Jahdu hollered in his meanest voice, "Hey, Uncle Calm Ocean! Why don't you once in a while get up and give the sand something to cool itself? Lying around all day, watering the clouds and cooling off the birds — Why don't you get yourself together long enough to help out the hot sand?"

Old Ocean wasn't bad. But he was used to being the biggest somebody around under the sky. He was used to not moving, just lying there as cool and blue as he pleased. Ocean knew he was bigger and wetter and deeper than anything under the sun. And when Jahdu said what he did, all grew still. The wind stopped its blowing. Ocean himself stopped being lazy long enough to think about what Jahdu said.

All at once Ocean gathered himself together right across his middle. He gave a heave that lifted his body higher than he had ever lifted it before. Ocean started moving from the horizon over the sand in a white, foaming line, treetop tall.

"Woogily!" said Jahdu. And he went on running.

Old Ocean leaped right in front of Jahdu. But he didn't catch Jahdu. No, he didn't. For Jahdu surely knew how to keep running along. Every time Ocean slid back to the horizon to gather himself together again, Jahdu would run away somewhere else. Ocean would hit the hot sand with all his might only to find that Jahdu had run by.

Jahdu laughed and laughed about it. "See? See?" Jahdu shouted to Ocean. "You've done a good thing for the sand. Now it will have a chance to cool itself once in a while."

Still today Ocean keeps moving up and back and up and back again. He keeps on trying to catch anything passing by.

How Jahdu Became a Boy

JAHDU was running eastward, for he had been born in the east. And now Jahdu thought he might like to be born into something else.

He was tired, and he felt like stopping to rest. But he had no friend he could stop along with. Jahdu had played so many tricks that nobody trusted him.

Mrs. Alligator used to give Jahdu free rides on her back. But not anymore. One time not long ago, Jahdu had come along with a can of blue paint on his head. He'd put Mrs. Alligator to sleep, and then he'd painted her blue. The paint hadn't worn off for a year. Now Mrs. Alligator thought Jahdu had manners worse than a crocodile's. Whenever she heard Jahdu running along, she would dive deep to the bottom of her pool. Yes, she would.

Jahdu came alongside a shade tree. The shade tree had leaves as big as elephants' ears. It had a trunk smooth to lean against. So Jahdu sat himself down. He leaned against the tree trunk and rested. He let the elephant-ear leaves fan him. He soon felt like taking a nap. He was almost asleep when he heard a voice next to him.

"Stranger, kindly move off my tail!" said the voice. "Hey, you, sir, who will lean against a body without a pardon me? Get yourself up!"

Jahdu jumped five feet away from the tree. "Woogily!" he said.

It wasn't the shade tree who had spoken. Shade trees rustle and sigh, but they've not been known to speak, and they don't care who leans against them. It was old Chameleon who had spoken. Chameleon was a lizard six inches long. He had not seen Jahdu for many a month. But when Jahdu said "Woogily!" Chameleon knew him right away.

"Jahdu," he said, "I wish you would learn to ask when you want to lean on somebody."

It took Jahdu a minute to see the lizard on the tree trunk. He smiled, for he'd always liked Chameleon. Chameleon could change the color of his skin any time he felt like it. And he never had to use paint to do it. If Chameleon sat down on a green leaf, he would turn himself green. Nobody could tell he was sitting on the leaf. If he wanted to sit on a flat stone, he would turn himself the color of the stone. And nobody need know he was resting there. Now Chameleon was brown, as was the dark brown tree trunk.

"Well, how you doing?" Jahdu asked, coming closer.

"You stay right where you are!" cried Chameleon. "Don't come nearer until you promise you won't tie my tail in a knot."

"Oh, my goodness," Jahdu said, sitting down.

"I mean what I say," Chameleon told Jahdu. "The last time you tied my tail up, I had an awful time getting it untied."

"How *did* you get it untied?" Jahdu wanted to know. He spoke to the lizard in his kindest voice. For Jahdu now wanted something special from him.

"Never you mind how I got myself loose," said Chameleon. "You just promise."

So Jahdu promised. Then he and Chameleon sat against the trunk of the shade tree.

"I've just been running along," Jahdu told him.

"All right," said Chameleon.

"I had a little fun with Grass," said Jahdu.

"That's good," said the lizard. "Grass is so gray and sad."

"Not anymore," Jahdu said. "Grass is now green as he can be."

"All right," Chameleon said. "Green is brighter than gray."

"I had a little fun with Ocean," Jahdu told his friend.

"That's all right, too," said Chameleon. "Ocean always did lie too far back on the horizon."

"Not anymore," Jahdu told him. "Now Ocean rises treetop tall. He runs over the hot sand hilltop high, and then he falls down trying to catch anything running along."

"That's good," said the lizard. "Now the hot sand will get a chance to cool itself."

"So I have stopped awhile from running along," said Jahdu.

"All right," Chameleon said.

"I stopped, and I know what I want from you," said Jahdu.

"Tell me then," said the lizard.

"I want to know how you work your magic," said Jahdu.

"You already have your own magic," Chameleon said. "You put things to sleep and wake them up again."

"But I need to know your magic as well."

"What magic is that?" asked Chameleon.

"You can change to look like a stone or even a leaf," Jahdu said.

"I can't let you do that," Chameleon said.

"I only want to know how it is you can change and hide," said Jahdu. "Then maybe I can learn how to just change into something else."

"Change into what?" Chameleon wanted to know.

"Into whatever I want," said Jahdu. "If I see a deer, I can be a deer running through the woods. If I see a fox, I can be as swift and clever as a fox."

Chameleon smiled. "It's not hard," he told Jahdu. "I will tell you what I do. With practice maybe it will work for you."

So Chameleon told him. And with a few shortcuts, Jahdu thought

Chameleon's magic would work for him. What he did was take Chameleon's magical words and fit them into his own words.

Jahdu left Chameleon dozing against the shade tree. He went running along eastward. He hadn't yet seen anything that he wanted to be.

"The first thing I see that I like, I will be," Jahdu said.

Soon he came to an island. The island had buildings higher than high. Jahdu liked the buildings. Yes, he did. "I'm going to make myself into a building!" he said.

He picked out a building higher than a hilltop.

"Word on!" he said, which was his way to begin changing into something. "Jahdu is running to that building. Jahdu is on top of that building. Jahdu *is* that building!"

From the word of Jahdu, he became a building made of steel and concrete. He was very tall, but he could not move. Jahdu did not like standing still.

"Woogily!" he said. And then, he thought quickly. "Word off!" he said. "Jahdu is jumping off this building. Jahdu is running away from this building. Jahdu is not a building anymore."

He went running on. Woogily! I have some more magic, he thought. He ran and he ran through the city on an island. He saw a stray cat, and he became the cat.

Jahdu Cat was always hungry. He was sick and tired, and he slept where he could. Jahdu Cat was thrown out of a supermarket for trying to catch a frozen fish for his supper.

"Cats have a hard time getting along. Word off!" Jahdu said. "Jahdu is jumping off this cat. Jahdu is running faster than this cat. Jahdu is not a cat anymore!"

Jahdu kept on running. He saw an orange-and-black taxicab.

"Woogily!" said Jahdu. "I'm going to be that taxicab." And so he was.

Now Jahdu was busy taking people from one place to another. People sat down hard on his seats. They tracked dirt on his floor. When he went fast, people shouted at him to slow down. Jahdu Taxi worked long hours. Yes, he did.

"Word off!" said Jahdu. "Jahdu is jumping off this taxicab. Jahdu is moving faster than this taxicab. Jahdu isn't a taxi anymore!"

He left the taxi at the curb and went running along. He found himself in a good place called Harlem. Most of the people there were warm shades of brown.

Jahdu came upon children playing. He saw a small black child having fun. "Word on!" he shouted. "Jahdu is running as fast as that child. Jahdu is jumping on him. Jahdu *is* that child!"

Black and brown were Jahdu's favorite colors, and Jahdu was now a strong black child. His name was Jahdu Lee Edward. He had a baseball but no bat. He had a dog. Yes, he did. The dog's name was Rufus. Jahdu Lee Edward had a sister and a brother, too.

"This is fun," he said to the other children. They played with him and Rufus. For a while Jahdu Lee Edward stayed in the neighborhood, enjoying himself. He had a good time in the city on an island.

JAHDU ADVENTURE

JAHDU ran through a field of bright flowers. He had left the good place called Harlem, the children, and Rufus. He was his own Jahdu self again. Yes, he was.

There was a low rumble of thunder from far away. Where there's thunder, there's lightning, thought Jahdu.

"I'm a streak of light!" he hollered, in a flash of feeling good. "I'm a trickmaker. I'm a painkiller, too. I'm Jahdu who is always running along!"

"You're a pain, all right. Poo-koo!" something said, from a distance away.

Nothing goes "Poo-koo," thought Jahdu. I must be hearing things.

He heard the sound again. It came from some mountains in the distance.

Jahdu looked all around and up at the sky. "Was that you, Great Blue, trying to talk to me?" he asked the sky.

"No, Jahdu," said the heavenly Blue.

"Well, how are you doing today?" Jahdu asked.

"I'm doing all right," said Great Blue, with a skywide smile.

"Good for you," Jahdu said.

Just then, Jahdu heard the strange sound coming closer. It went, "Poo-koo, poo-koo," at Jahdu.

"Poo-*koo?* Humph!" said Jahdu. "What a silly sound!"

"Wa-ka-ta poo-koo," the sound went, closer still.

"What?" said Jahdu.

"I said 'wa-ka-ta poo-koo.'" A shiny thing about the size of Jahdu came up to him out of the sunlight in the bright field. It seemed to be a robot made of metal. "How are you, Jahdu?" it asked. It clanged all around.

"Woogily!" said Jahdu. "I'm fine. What are you? Where are you going? How in the world do you know my name?"

"Poo-koo. Well," said the thing, "everybody knows Jahdu who is always running along. Wa-ka-ta."

"That's the truth," said Jahdu, proudly. "The whole world knows me. But who are you?"

"We haven't met in a while," said the shiny thing, clanging loudly. "But you must remember me. I'm the giant Trouble. I've come to pay you a visit. Is this where you live?"

"No, it isn't," Jahdu said. "I live atop a gum tree. Anyway, you are a size small, just like me. You are no giant Trouble."

"Wa-ka-ta poo-koo!" said the metal thing. "Oh, yes, I am. I'm the big one called Trouble."

Jahdu cartwheeled out of the way of the rolling, clanging thing.

"Trouble has legs as long as highways," said Jahdu. "And feet as big as ships of the sea."

"Wa-ka-ta," purred the thing moving along toward the mountains. "I have ship-feet and highway-legs without end."

"No you don't!" cried Jahdu. "Anyone can see you are much too small to be a giant. And Trouble has a gold loop as bright as the moon through his ear. There is a barrel the size of a standpipe hanging from the loop."

"I've got a gold earring," said the thing. "See? It has a blue barrel hanging from it."

Sure enough, Jahdu saw that the shiny thing wore a tiny earring bolted to its tin ear. Hanging from it was a barrel the size of a teeny blue bead.

"You might be a little bit of Trouble," Jahdu said, "but you are not any giant."

"Oh, yes I am!" squeaked the thing. It crouched in front of Jahdu.

"Would you care to wrestle to see who can win?" asked Jahdu.

But the shiny thing only shouted, *"I'm the giant Trouble! I'm bigger than fifty-two mountains!"*

Wait a minute, Jahdu thought. Why, that fits the giant to a T-rouble. Trouble *is* as big as a whole mountain range. Oh-oh, now it's time to be careful!

The thing clanged and rolled toward the mountains. It whirled its arms. It creaked and whistled. It hollered: *"I'm Trouble! The fifty-two giant. Bigger than mountains!* Wa-ka-poo yay!"

"Woogily!" whispered Jahdu. He followed out of harm's way.

"Gi-ant!" the thing shouted. It swayed. Its voice slowed down. *"Biiig Trouble!"* it said, its voice growing slower and deeper. *"Fif . . . fif . . . yay . . ."*

"You sound like a windup toy running down," Jahdu said.

The shiny thing fell over on its head at the foot of the mountain range. It hummed for a moment. Then, it was quiet.

All at once, a giant hand swooped down from up high. It caught the little shiny thing and Jahdu in one grasp.

"How you doing, Jahdu?" came a mighty voice from above.

"I was doing all right until just now," said Jahdu.

"Ho, Ho, Ho," came the huge laugh. It was Trouble, for sure. There he was, lying in wait across the landscape. He looked like a whole mountain range.

"How did you like my windup toy?" Trouble asked.

"It fooled me," said Jahdu. "I had to follow to see where it would go."

"I figured you would," said Trouble.

"You tricked me good," Jahdu said. "But, please, don't put me back in your barrel. I'm so afraid of being in there."

"*Ho!*" laughed Trouble. "I'm going to put you there, Jahdu. It's where I keep my shiny double, Trouble, too."

The left hand of Trouble tipped the barrel on his earring. The right hand of Trouble dropped Jahdu—plop!—and the shiny toy Trouble—clang!—to the bottom of the barrel. And Jahdu smiled. Yes, he did.

The huge barrel of Trouble was full of babies, donkeys, lions, and birds, plus a tiger, a cow, a horse, a hiker, a biker, and plenty of rabbits.

"How's everybody?" asked Jahdu.

"It's Jahdu!" said Striper Tiger. "The giant has caught Jahdu. We're in trouble for sure!"

"We're getting out of here," Jahdu told everybody.

"But how?" asked Brown Cow.

Jahdu thought about it. "Well, maybe it will take time," he said. "But when the time comes, everybody must do what I tell them."

"We will!" said everybody.

"Good!" said Jahdu.

He sat down next to the shiny toy and took out all of its bolts and springs. He broke off the windup key and threw out some of the parts.

"Hide this junk in the barrel's cracks," Jahdu told everybody. "Keep up your screams and cries. They're the sounds Trouble likes best."

The blue barrel swayed on the earring that pierced Trouble's ear.

"Ooooh! Ahhh-ooooo!" went the crying out loud that was music to the giant. Screams and cries put him to sleep.

Night fell, and a silver moon came up.

"Trouble will sleep until I'm ready for him to wake up," said Jahdu. He had finished his work on the shiny toy. "Quiet!" he told everybody.

Everybody quit crying out loud. The silence woke Trouble. He sat up like a mountain range moving. His barrel swayed, as big as a blue sun in the moonlight.

"What happened to the noise I like to hear?" asked Trouble.

Silence.

He unclipped the barrel and sat it upon his knee. There was everybody, lying on the floor. The shiny toy was sprawled in the middle.

But there was no sign of Jahdu.

"Where's he hiding?" roared Trouble. He emptied everybody and his toy on the ground. Slowly, everybody stood up.

The shiny toy swayed. Suddenly, it whirled in a silvery dance under the moon.

The giant Trouble was enchanted. He forgot the shiny thing wasn't a real live dancer. He forgot that Jahdu was nowhere to be found.

The shiny toy robot circled Trouble's feet. It led everybody in a fairy dance, light as air, into the field. Soon, everybody was on the far, far side, and running fast, away.

Only the shiny toy stood silvery still. "Hal-loo, look over here! Guess who?" it called to Trouble. Out from inside the toy popped Jahdu.

"That's who!" He bowed to Trouble. And his laughter filled the air.

The great right hand of Trouble swooped down. It missed Jahdu by a fingernail.

"I won't get much sleep without the screaming and crying sounds I like to hear," said Trouble.

"So, you get paid back for tricking folks," Jahdu told him.

"Without sleep, I won't feel like finding something to eat," whimpered the giant.

"Try eating the moon," said Jahdu. He laughed. "It's hanging up there, just above you."

Trouble would try anything once. He leaped for the moon and caught it. The moon was heavy, and Trouble dropped it.

"Look out below!" Jahdu cried.

The silver moon fell right on Trouble's foot. Yes, it did.

"Ow-wow!" hollered Trouble.

"Well, it serves you right," said Jahdu. "But anyway, I have to leave you now."

"You took all my company away," said the giant, rubbing his big toe. "And you didn't even say good night."

"Woogily!" said Jahdu. "All of a sudden, you sound like a moping, pouting giant."

"I'm not so bad," said Trouble. "I do what I do, is all."

"Well, if you're not so bad, and if you still want a good night from me, you'd better promise to put the moon back," Jahdu told him.

"I promise," said the giant.

"And promise not to make another clanging thing," said Jahdu.

"I promise not to," said Trouble.

"Don't believe him," said everybody. They came up, hiding behind Jahdu.

"Well, we'll see if Trouble is a little bit friendly, too," said Jahdu.

Trouble put the moon back among the stars. "There," he said.

"Good!" said Jahdu.

Then Trouble flattened his silvery toy and clipped it like a buckle to his belt.

"That looks nice!" Jahdu told him.

Everybody and Jahdu showed the giant how to find field greens in the moonlight and cook them under the stars. They gathered grasses, built a fire in the barrel, and used the shiny thing as a grill.

"Ummm, good!" said the giant when the field greens were cooked.

Then Jahdu said, "Good night!" to the giant. And they all left Trouble happily eating under the moon.

Jahdu called good-bye and went on running. But whenever he came upon mountains, he would say, "There lies Trouble!" and he'd run the other way.

J AHDU was running along, just playing around in the woods. And he was singing as loud as he knew how.

Birdy Robin was there in a sweet gum tree, giving her children their dinner. "Stop making so much noise, Jahdu," Birdy Robin said. "You are upsetting my young'uns."

"Oh, hush, Birdy," Jahdu answered. "I like to sing—Tra-la, tra-la—hear? My voice is such a singable sound. And I will sing whenever I want to."

And so Jahdu did.

> *"I'm singing in the woods-dim,*
> *In the sun-hot and the shade-cool.*
> *Oh, I'm singing to the sky-high*
> *And anywhere else I've a mind to. . ."*

There began a screeching at Jahdu from the woodpeckers and cardinals, little sparrows, too. And from blackbirds and chickadees and blue jays.

"Jahdu, you are spoiling the woods for everybody," all the birds told him. "Please go running somewhere else. We don't want you singing badly under our trees."

Oh, that made Jahdu angry. Yes, it did. He stuck out his face. He squeezed his eyes shut and threw his voice at the nearest bothersome bird.

"Sapsuckers are ugly as mud," said the black-capped chickadee.

"What did you say about me, Chickie?" asked the yellow-bellied sapsucker.

"I said, sapsuckers like you are ugly as wet, burnt kindling," said the chickadee.

Chickie was so shocked at what seemed to come out of her mouth that she fell from her branch. She went *plop!* on an anthill. In no time, a line of furious ants were crawling over her.

"I hope they chew your feathers into fluff!" said the sapsucker.

"Off me! Off me!" Chickie hollered, flicking ants every which way with her wing tips.

Jahdu stuck out his face again and squeezed his eyes shut. He threw his voice at the cardinal this time. *"Blue jays are the foulest birds,"* said

Big Red Cardinal. *"Jays fuss about nothing. They have no manners. We should name them blue blups, they are so silly-looking."*

"Watch it! Watch it, you!" Crester Blue Jay chattered. "What are *you* doing here, Red?" he asked the cardinal. "You belong in a thicket anyhow, or a garden. Get out of our woods!"

"Yes, get out of our woods!" yelled all of the birds at Big Red.

Big Red Cardinal screeched in fear at what had come from his mouth a moment ago. He thought there must be someone else living inside him. He flew away, screaming all the way to his thicket.

Jahdu laughed and laughed. By throwing his voice and saying awful things, he had scared the birds and caused them to fight amongst themselves. That's what they get for telling *him* to go away.

Jahdu had spoken in his usual voice while throwing it. But he knew to muffle the tones. And he let the air out of his mouth very slowly. He kept his mouth as closed as he could. And only the tip of his tongue moved inside. It made his voice seem not like his at all. It made it different, and higher, so it sounded like somebody else. That's how Jahdu threw it. And he was quite good at it, too.

Jahdu ran away from the birds. He went on and on until he had to slow down. For there was something ahead of him. It was a whole line of things sliding sleekly and steadily along toward him. They had heads like black teardrops. Below each head was a black, skinny stem.

Woogily! They remind me of something, thought Jahdu. But he couldn't think what.

The things didn't even look at Jahdu. They were slipping by without a word and humming in one boring tone as they went.

"Humph," Jahdu muttered. He stuck up his face and threw his voice at them. It smacked into the funny things going by. Yes, it did.

"Ugly things," the things seemed to say about themselves. *"We look like a parade of knots with dirty strings hanging down. We look like nothing worth anything!"*

All of a sudden, the black knots spun around in a line. They seemed to look at Jahdu, and they never stopped moving and humming. Until they did something Jahdu never thought possible. All of them sounded just like Jahdu!

"Pretty things," they said in Jahdu's voice.

Hey, how did you do that? Jahdu wanted to say to the skinny things. But when he opened his mouth, nothing came out.

Help! Help! Jahdu tried to say. But he had no sound in his throat.

I can't talk. Help! Crester! Big Red! Somebody! I can't talk! Jahdu tried to speak, but no sound came.

"Poor Jahdu," sang the things in Jahdu's voice. They swooped around him in racing, trilling Jahdu sound. The faster they went, the quicker they looked, like speeded-up dots with stems.

After a second Jahdu understood they were singing things to him. *"Who do you think you are, Jahdu?"* the things sang. *"We took your voice, and now we'll take you!"*

Oh, no! Wait! thought voiceless Jahdu.

The things linked themselves together. Lines stretched across the bottom of the stems. More lines stretched above the bottom one — a second and a third one. They fenced Jahdu in on every side. And they put his voice in a voice box inside the fence with him.

All of this time, Jahdu was speechless. He'd lost his voice, but he hadn't lost his mind. He was thinking fast.

Now I know what they are. Yes! thought Jahdu. Notes of music! They were quarter notes when I first saw them slipping by, one step at a time.

But now they are faster, Jahdu thought. Now they are joined. *Beaming* — that's what it's called.

Jahdu studied the notes of music that had fenced him in. He saw that they were thirty-second notes. For they had three beam lines across the note stems.

They mean to take me prisoner, Jahdu thought to himself. And I always liked music, too. But not so fast!

Jahdu kept his wits about him. Yes, he did. And he had thought of a plan.

Help! Help! he hollered, with no sound at all. Let me out! He cringed and trembled. He made it seem that he was awfully afraid. But of course, he wasn't. He was Jahdu.

Jahdu is getting out from behind these bars, he thought. He began running very fast inside the cage the thirty-second notes had made.

Jahdu dust rose out of Jahdu and fell on the highest beam connecting the notes. The beam yawned. It fell down, sound asleep.

Without the highest beam, the notes slowed down to sixteenth notes like this:

Jahdu kept on running, and his magic dust fell everywhere. Part of the second beam fell. There was a scattering of eighth notes, like this:

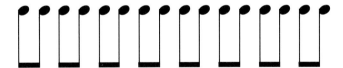

"Oh-oh," hummed the notes, yawning. *"What . . . is happ . . . 'ning to . . . us?"*

Woogily! thought Jahdu. He grabbed his voice from the voice box beside him.

"Woogily! Glad to be going home!" his voice said softly to him, as Jahdu let it slip down his throat.

"I'm a streak of light," Jahdu whispered. He didn't want the notes to know just yet that he had his voice back.

Jahdu ran back and forth some more. Jahdu dust rose like a fog and fell over the beams holding the eighth notes together. The beams fell to the ground. The notes separated. Now they became quarter notes. They looked like this:

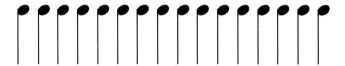

The quarter notes were so sleepy and tired that they shriveled and *rested* like this:

The rests were light as feathers. Jahdu shoved them aside.

"There!" he said. "I'm free!"

The quarter rests quivered, but they stayed silent. They were too weak to move much.

I couldn't put them fast asleep, Jahdu was thinking. Even the rests in music have a lot of power.

"So, good-bye, all you notes-no-more," Jahdu said, getting out of there. "Fool around in the woods, if you want to. Just remember Jahdu. And you'd better never ever again fool around with me!"

After that Jahdu was careful about throwing his voice. In fact, he kept it to himself. But most birds of the woods wouldn't have anything to do with him for a long, long time.

"Oh, well," Jahdu said one day to his friend, Chameleon, to whom he told most things. "There are places to see and things to do."

"And there always will be," said Chameleon.

"I'm a trickmaker. I'm a streak of light," boasted Jahdu. "I'm the one-and-only Jahdu there is!"

"Thank goodness for that!" said Chameleon.

And that's the Jahdu truth.

How Jahdu Uncovered CIGAM

JAHDU was running along. He had awakened on the wrong side of his black gum tree.

"Something doesn't feel right," he said out loud. Now, he looked all around as he ran. He was in a glen. He didn't know his way at all. For he hadn't had the time yet to run around the glen.

Just then, Jahdu saw a wing-low bird flying his way. The low-flyer knocked some lacy wugs off the roll-along weeds. The spidery, lacy wugs had fan shapes like sails along their backs. The breeze from a wing-low passing by knocked them over.

"Woogily!" said Jahdu. "I'll have me some fun."

Jahdu caught the wing-low by its tail feather and wrestled the fluffy, pea-green bird to the ground. The lacy wugs sailed away as Jahdu jumped up and ran faster and faster around the fallen wing-low. Jahdu dust rose out of Jahdu and fell on the bird. Yes, it did.

"Jahdu, son, you act *sooo* foolish," said the wing-low bird. He flapped his wings to get all the dust off.

"Why aren't you asleep?" asked Jahdu. "My dust is *strong* and can put you to sleep."

"Silly Jahdu," said the wing-low bird. "You have lost something, and you don't know it." The wing-low sprang to its bright red feet and flew away.

"I haven't lost a thing that I know of," said Jahdu. His dust rose up off the ground and fell back into Jahdu again.

Jahdu went right on running. He came upon that Lee Edward child walking his dog, Rufus.

Where did he come from? Jahdu wondered. All of a sudden, he felt like becoming Lee Edward again. Yes, he did.

"How you doing, Lee Edward?" asked Jahdu. He came up fast.

"Doing all right," said Lee Edward. He didn't much trust Jahdu, who he heard had been playing more tricks on folks.

All at once, Jahdu began shouting. "Word on! Jahdu is coming as fast as Lee Edward is going. Jahdu is jumping on Lee Edward's shoulders. Jahdu *is* the child, Lee Edward!"

"Jahdu, dummy, get down off my shoulders!" hollered Lee Edward.

Rufus leaped high and bit a chunk out of Jahdu. Rufus spat out the chunk. He coughed and sneezed at the taste of Jahdu.

"Lee Edward, I should've *become* you, just the way Chameleon taught me to. But I didn't," said Jahdu.

"Silly Jahdu," said Lee Edward, "you've lost something, and you don't know it." He and his dog, Rufus, ran away. Yes, they did.

"I haven't lost anything that I know of," Jahdu said to himself. And he

boasted, "I'm a streak of light! I'm a trickmaker! I'm Jahdu just running through."

"Does hollering out loud make you feel better, little Jahdu-silly?" asked a careful voice.

Jahdu jumped treetop high. Yes, he did. "Woogily! You scared me," he said. "Who in the world is running with me?"

"Just me," said the careful voice. The gray shape of it ran alongside Jahdu.

"Oh, right," said Jahdu. "Now I see, you're my shadow."

Shadow did two flips in midair.

"You're supposed to do what *I* do!" said Jahdu. "How did you do something like that?"

But Shadow wouldn't say. Instead, he asked, "How you doing, Jahdu?"

"Doing all right," Jahdu told him. He didn't much like having his shadow run loose.

"Everybody is saying you've lost something, and that you don't know it," said Shadow, hopping along.

"Haven't lost a thing," said Jahdu.

"I hear you lost your power!" said Shadow, doing cartwheels.

"Did not," snapped Jahdu.

"Don't lie," said Shadow. "You have a hard time putting anything to sleep. You've lost your power, and I know who has it, too." Shadow leaped high. He sailed over Jahdu's head.

"You know who has my magic?" asked Jahdu.

"The Shadow knows everything," said Shadow. "I was there when your magic power was taken."

"Please tell me who has my power," Jahdu said.

"What will you give me if I do?" Shadow asked.

"This kick in the pants!" Jahdu yelled. But he missed Shadow by a hairsbreadth. He nearly knocked his own self down.

"Don't get so pooft and pahft," said Shadow.

"Then tell me who took my power," Jahdu said.

"Oh, Jahdu of the Jahdu dust!" chanted Shadow. "Your power was taken by The Greatest Somebody in the whole wide world."

"But The Greatest Somebody in the whole wide world is *me,*" Jahdu said.

"Not anymore. The Greatest Somebody is my friend, C I G A M," Shadow said.

"S E E - J A M ?"

"Spelled C-I-G-A-M," said Shadow.

"Never heard of him," Jahdu said.

"It doesn't matter," said Shadow. "It's C I G A M who has your power."

Jahdu lunged for his shadow. But Shadow sidestepped him.

"C I G A M stole your power while you slept," Shadow went on. "He took it beyond the horizon. But you must never, ever, never go there."

"Why?" asked Jahdu, jumping up and down. He was growing tired of Shadow.

"Because if you go there, C I G A M will whirl you in a wind," Shadow said. "He will burn you with hot coals and plant asparagus up your nose! Oh, he's The Greatest Somebody in the whole wide world!"

Jahdu stepped on his shadow and jumped up and down on it. Shadow slid up and shoved Jahdu to the ground. They wrestled that way like two cranky children. They wrestled until it grew dark.

"I beat you out of sight, Shadow," Jahdu said.

"Jahdu-silly, I'll see you in the morning," Shadow answered, and he disappeared.

In the morning, Jahdu was running along. Shadow ran along with him. Jahdu paid him no mind, and Shadow paid no attention to Jahdu.

When finally Jahdu came to the horizon, he rolled up the sky and crawled under.

Shadow scrambled under the sky, too. "You're in for it now, Jahdu!" Shadow said, and he ran away.

Jahdu watched the sky roll back down to meet the horizon again. This is something! he thought. It's like being backstage. I bet this is where the day and night go on.

Sure enough, behind the scenes, the day spilled out over the morning. The night was black and full in a mighty dark cup. Jahdu climbed the cup and stuck his finger in the night full of stars to taste it. Gently he touched a star. It was slippery and hot.

Jahdu jumped down and ran along backstage. He was surprised to find Grass there, growing browner by the hour. Grass's dry roots pointed up in the air.

"Woogily!" said Jahdu. "What is going on? Why is everything all mixed-up?"

He came to a swamp and caught sight of Mrs. Alligator. She was belly-up in the mossy water, kicking and shaking.

"Woogily!" whispered Jahdu. He didn't know where he was going, but he hurried along anyway. Soon, he came to a place full of possums and catbirds and bees.

"Hey, everybody!" Jahdu shouted. "What's the matter with you? Why are you upside down just like Grass and Mrs. Alligator? And where's The Greatest Nobody keeping itself?"

Everybody stayed quiet in the worst kind of kicking-and-shaking sleep. Yes, they did.

But someone was moving along. It was a figure turned backward, and it was coming toward Jahdu.

"What's that?" Jahdu asked.

"Aarwrrag!" said the figure with its back to him. "Grrogg! You're not welcome here, little Jahdu-silly. So get going!" The someone flung a piece of shimmer over its shoulder at Jahdu like a net to trap him.

"I don't feel like being captured today," Jahdu said. He scrambled out from under the net. "I know who you are," Jahdu said. "You're C I G A M, The Greatest *Nobody* anywhere!"

But the shimmer stuck itself to Jahdu. It felt soft and warm, like his own self. "Ohhhh!" sighed Jahdu. It *was* part of his own self!

"Wait until I catch you, Jahdu-silly," hollered the figure. "Aarwrrag!"

"What did you call me again?" asked Jahdu.

"Called you Jahdu-silly, which you are," said the figure. "And what will you do about it, little Jahdu-silly?"

"Ho, ho!" laughed Jahdu. "I'll show you what I'm going to do!"

He reeled in the shimmer. The figure began to unravel. *"Please don't do that,"* begged the figure. It spun around in circles.

And in no time Jahdu had a round ball of shimmer. Yes, he did. "I didn't know what this was at first," he said. "I've never been without it before." He saw that the shimmer was his own Jahdu magic power. "I know!" he said. "Hmmmmm. C-I-G-A-M . . . spelled . . . backward — M-A-G-I-C! C I G A M is my M A G I C spelled backward! And I know who the figure is, too. You're Shadow — *my* shadow!

"Shadow, you used my magic upside down and roundabout," Jahdu went on. "You wrapped yourself in it and called yourself C I G A M. You're the one that's silly!"

Jahdu ran faster and faster around Shadow. His dust fell all over Shadow. Full of magic again, the Jahdu dust put Shadow in a deep sleep. There was no kicking in it and no shaking anywhere.

Just then, everybody woke up. They turned right side up and began cheering Jahdu. "Hurray for The Greatest *Somebody* in the whole wide world!" everybody said.

Jahdu took a tiny piece of power from his shimmer ball of magic. He stuck it deep inside Shadow. Ever so slowly, he ran around Shadow.

Jahdu dust rose out of Shadow and fell back into Jahdu.

Shadow woke up. Yes, he did.

"Where am I?" he mumbled.

"You're with me," Jahdu told him. "You're my shadow attached to me, the way you're supposed to be."

"Oh, me," groaned his shadow.

Shadow was very dim when Jahdu went running along. Jahdu unwound his magic as he ran. He flung it around him like a cloak, for the cup of night was now pouring in a cool, dark spill.

Shimmering on a star stream, Jahdu and Shadow slipped away. Jahdu lifted up the sky from the horizon and slipped under and out again.

"That was sure something!" he said, watching the sky roll back down. His cloak of magic dust fell away deep inside him.

Shadow was right there, almost invisible, but he didn't say a word. He was planning his escape.

And that's the U D H A J truth,

Till this good day becomes . . . W O R R O M O T .

Jahdu in the Far Woods

J AHDU went on running through a sparkly day.

He ran, jumping from one pool of light through the trees to the next. He spun himself around and around, leaping high each time. When Jahdu stopped a moment, he looked up to see Great Blue Sky spinning with him.

"How you doing today, Great Blue?" Jahdu called up.

"Doing all right, Jahdu," said Great Blue. "You turn so fast, you make

me spin-dizzy, too. Better watch yourself, though. You are now in a far woods."

"I'm not afraid," said Jahdu. "Is this a new place I haven't been?"

"It's a very old place," said Great Blue.

"I must know it, then," said Jahdu. "But I'll be careful, too."

Tall trees with their sweeping branches closed out most of the sparkly light. All of the brightness faded from the sunny day. Soft hues were left — yellows and purples, some green and brown, too. It all made Jahdu feel odd.

"Where's everybody?" he whispered to himself.

"Hal-loo," he called and listened for his echo. "*Ooh-ooh-ooh . . .*" was what came back. The sound made him shiver. "Woogily!" Jahdu said softly.

The trees pressed close all around. Jahdu was alone. He yawned, for the quiet light made him sleepy. He saw he was on a path.

Why, I bet this is the good-and-bad path to Sweetdream and Nightmare, still growing on the banyan tree! This might not be a far woods at all, Jahdu thought. I remember, I made all kinds of things grow to cover the path. . . . Where am I?

Jahdu couldn't tell where he was. All was strange now. Before him the path was like a thicket. He thought there might be a banyan tree on the other side. He thought he'd go see.

Jahdu scrambled through the thicket. He didn't find the banyan tree. What he saw took his breath away.

In front of him was a clearing in the shadowy woods. And in the clearing was the prettiest gingerbread house he could hope to see. It looked good enough to eat. It *was* good enough to eat. For it was made out of sweets and bread and cookies.

There were candy-cane windows and a chocolate-drop chimney. The sides of the house were lengths of baked gingerbread, iced with chocolate. The roof was made out of chunks of red taffy, edged with gingersnaps.

There were gumdrops and fudge chunkys and all-day suckers every-where.

"Woogily!" Jahdu said.

What he saw next made him shout. Yes, it did.

"Well, look who's here!" shouted Jahdu. "How you doing, Hansel? Hey Gretel, what do you say!"

Hansel and Gretel stood eating part of a candy cane.

"We found it, and you can't have any," Gretel said, about the candy-sweet house. She didn't even say hello to Jahdu.

"But what are you doing here?" asked Jahdu.

"What are *you* doing here?" asked Hansel. "You're in the wrong woods, Jahdu."

"I go anywhere I want," said Jahdu, proudly. And then, "How did you know my name?"

"Stories are told about you," said Gretel. The children turned away, their mouths and pockets full of candy. Then the shiny, white, sweet door of the house swung open. An old woman stood there, smiling at the children and waving them inside. At once, Hansel and Gretel followed her.

"Wait!" cried Jahdu. "Don't go in there. The old woman is a—"

The shiny door slammed in Jahdu's face, spraying icing everywhere.

"—witch," he finished. If I remember right, thought Jahdu, the witch wanted to eat Hansel for supper. But Gretel tricked the witch and pushed *her* into the oven. Imagine! The gingerbread house made of goodies right here. Hansel and Gretel, too. And I saw all of it.

Jahdu gathered a handful of gumdrops to eat on his way through the far woods. This wasn't like any place he'd ever been. Everything seemed enchanted, all silvery and gold now, full of sparkles again and streams of pretty colors.

Out of a rainbow stream like a waterfall spilling through an opening in the air came Little Red Riding Hood.

Jahdu stopped still. "I know you!" he hollered, gulping down three gumdrops at once, he was so excited.

"Jahdu, please, not so loud. You must be rather careful in the far woods," said Little Red Riding Hood.

"But . . . how do you know me?" stammered Jahdu. "Be careful of what — the big, bad wolf?"

"Him, of course," said Red Riding Hood, "as well as other dangers. What are *you* doing here, Jahdu?"

"I'm on my way home, but I somehow got turned around. I mean, everything is changed," said Jahdu. "And how is it you know who I am?"

"I know you the way you know me," said Red Riding Hood. "And I suspect you are lost."

"I am," said Jahdu. "And I wish I knew how to get back home."

"Well, keep along this path. There's a prince up ahead who may be able to help you. If not him, then the woodsman. Good-bye, Jahdu."

"Wait!" cried Jahdu. "If you're on your way to your grandmother's house, please don't go there!"

"I have to go," said Riding Hood. "Grandmother needs me today. She's not feeling well."

"No . . . the wolf," began Jahdu.

But Red Riding Hood walked along a rainbow stream. Jahdu couldn't see, the light dazzled so. When his sight cleared, the stream had vanished. And so had Little Red Riding Hood.

"Woogily!" said Jahdu. "This *is* an odd place. I'd better find the woodsman. I can't remember the whole story, but I think he has to help Red Riding Hood."

Jahdu went running along as fast as he could. He slowed to a trot when he came upon a fine prince trying to chop down a wall of thorny briers.

"Hello, Sir Prince. Nice to see you today!"

The prince didn't stop laboring. "Good day, Jahdu. I see you've gotten lost in the far woods."

"Well, I do seem to be in the middle of things," said Jahdu. "I must find the woodsman. Red Riding Hood is going to run into the big, bad wolf at her grandmother's house. Would you like to help?"

"I would if I could," said the prince. "But Sleeping Beauty is fast asleep on the other side of this wall of thorny briers. And I must try to wake her before nightfall."

"How long has she been asleep?" asked Jahdu.

"Oh, about thirty years," said the prince.

"What happens if you don't wake her up before nightfall?" asked Jahdu.

"Another day will be lost," said the prince, "while Sleeping Beauty sleeps on. And if I were you, Jahdu, I'd get to your woods before dark."

"Oh, I will," said Jahdu. "If I can just figure out how."

"Perhaps the chicken can help you," the prince said.

"Who's the chicken?" Jahdu asked.

"She's the hip-hop bird. Behind you," said the prince, and went on with his chopping work.

Jahdu turned to see. Behind him stood a red hen, as big and wide as a summer sunset.

ELLO, JAHDU," said the hen. The sound of her knocked Jahdu down.

"OH, SORRY! I mean, I'm so sorry," said the hen, more softly.

"Halloooo," Jahdu called, picking himself up. "I've never seen a hen before with her head in the clouds." The chicken looked to be a half-a-mile tall.

She clucked a chuckle and blew clouds out of sight. Lowering her head to Jahdu, she said, "Just call me Cackle G. The G stands for Giant." And she gave out a cackle, not too loud.

"Cackle G., I'm pleased to meet you," said Jahdu. "But the far woods seems like a storybook place, and I don't remember you in any tale."

"That's because I'm not in one, yet," said Cackle G. "But I hope some-day somebody will like to tell about me."

"What is it that you've done?" asked Jahdu.

"Well, I'm still a young hen, and I haven't done much," she said. "There isn't a fox in the far woods that will try to carry me off, I'm so *big*. My dad is ordinary size, and my mom is Chicken Little, you know. And they're afraid I will step on them or blow them over."

"I don't wonder," said Jahdu.

"When I cackle loud, I can make a herd of deer flip over," Cackle G.

went on. "If I scratch for food, I dig canyons and rivers in the ground. So you can see how hard it is for me to have done a whole story."

"I do see. But maybe I can help you," said Jahdu.

"Oh, I hope so! Do you have something for me to do?" asked Cackle G.

"If you can get me home, I'll tell everybody the story of how you did it," Jahdu said.

"Wonderful! Where do you live?" asked Cackle G.

"I live in a black gum tree on the Mountain of Paths where all the little animals walk. My friends are often upset with me because I play tricks," said Jahdu. "But I am sure they are worried because they don't know where I am. I was running and turning around and around. And Great Blue said I made him dizzy."

"That's where we'll start. We'll ask Great Blue about it," said Cackle G.

"Oh, but I forgot," said Jahdu. "I was on my way to get the woodsman to help Little Red Riding Hood."

"Never mind," said the chicken, G. "I've tried to help Little Red. I offered her rides and promised to step on that bad wolf for her. But she told me, 'Mind your own story, G.'

"The woodsman rescues her and her grandmother every time," G. said. "That's the way things are in the far woods." The big chicken sighed, causing a whirlwind for twenty minutes.

"Woogily!" said Jahdu, when the wind was spent.

"Everybody here has a story, except me," finished Cackle G. And then she rested her huge head in some evergreens and closed her eyes.

"I see," said Jahdu. "But don't you worry. We'll find you a story. And don't be sad. First let's start by visiting Great Blue."

Suddenly, G. was out of the piny woods and feeling better. "Climb aboard," she said. "We'll talk to Great Blue up close, see what he knows."

Jahdu climbed up on Cackle G.'s foot. "I didn't know chickens could fly to the sky, but I guess giant hens can do anything they want."

"What I do looks like flying," said Cackle G. "Mainly, I do a hip-hop up. Then I spread my wings and glide. It's more like making leapfrogs with coasting in between the leap and the frog. It's that I'm so big . . ."

"I understand," said Jahdu. "Whew!" He hadn't reached the chicken's thigh joint yet, and he'd been climbing for a while. He clung to some short feathers, trying to catch his breath.

"Here, let me help," said Cackle G. She took little Jahdu in her beak. G. turned her head to the side; her beak dangled Jahdu. Then she flung him up and up. Yes, she did.

Jahdu flipped three times and landed on the giant bird's back.

"Woogily!" said Jahdu. He settled in. "This is like floating on a fluffy red ocean high in the air!"

The chicken clucked loudly and knocked down a mile of thorny briers.

"Thanks!" called the charming prince, still laboring away. He high-jumped over the thorns on his way to wake up Sleeping Beauty.

"Good-bye!" Jahdu called to him. He was holding on tight. For Cackle G. had begun hip-hopping. In one great hip-hop of a takeoff, they were floating up toward Great Blue. Well, it was like floating. Each flap of Cackle G.'s wings took a good half hour up and a half hour down.

"Talk fast," said the chicken to Jahdu. "I can't coast up here forever."

"I was turning around and around," Jahdu explained to the blue sky.

"And I said, 'Jahdu, you make me dizzy,'" said Great Blue.

"You told me to be careful because I was in a far woods," Jahdu went on.

Said old Blue, "You turned around and around *left* when you should have turned around and around *right*. You must never go left when turning around and around, unless you want to find yourself in some other place."

"I see," said Jahdu. "Thank you, Great Blue."

The hip-hop ride had taken them high up toward Blue. Now, the gliding and coasting brought them back down to the far woods' ground.

"I see how you do it," said Jahdu. "And if I turn around and around to the right, I should get to my woods again."

"That leaves me out," said the big chicken, sadly.

"Oh, but I owe you more of a story, don't I?" Jahdu said. "So why don't I stay on your back and hold on tight . . ."

"While I turn around and around to the right!" said Cackle G.

"Perfect!" Jahdu agreed.

Having Cackle G. along made things a bit different. The giant chicken turned around and around to the right. She spun, hipping in the air, in her hopping style. And away she and Jahdu flew for as long as a ride takes from a fanciful spin. They sailed along, seeing the sights. They passed a giant eagle, with passengers.

"Those riders must have spun around the wrong way, too," said Jahdu.

"And caught a ride with the biggest eagle in the sky," added Cackle G.

There were lots of well-known story folks going places. Jahdu saw John Henry with his hammer in his hand. There was John the Conqueror, the hope-bringer, feeding the eagle as it flew. He was a giant of a man, even bigger than big John Henry.

"Two Johns, howdy-do!" called Cackle G. Both big Johns waved.

"Halloooo!" Jahdu called and waved, himself.

There were animals riding the eagle. Bruh Rabbit had been fast asleep, using a soft feather as a blanket. He wiggled his ears at the sound of G. cackling along. Bruh Rabbit raised his head and sniffled his nose. Then he waved a foot at Jahdu.

"Bruh Rabby, hallooo!" Jahdu called. "Never thought I'd see you in person!"

"I wonder what far woods that lickety-split Bruh Rabby lives in?" Jahdu called to the chicken.

"Maybe next time you spin around the wrong way, you'll find out," said Cackle G.

The big chicken waved a wing. The eagle waved back. So did the Knee-High Man, who was so small Jahdu almost missed seeing him. And there was the Hairy Toe and the Hairy Man, sitting far out on one of the eagle's wings, all by themselves.

Jahdu nodded to them, though they did make a chill go through him. The Hairy Man stared at the great hen, and Jahdu saw that the Hairy Toe was watching, too. He just wasn't sure which part of the Hairy Toe was looking. Neither the Hairy Toe nor the Hairy Man greeted the hen or Jahdu, either.

"Woogily!" whispered Jahdu. "I wouldn't want to meet *them* in a far woods after dark."

Cackle G. came down pretty fast atop the Mountain of Paths in Jahdu's own woods. All the little animals had scurried for cover when an alarm was given. "The sky is falling! The sky is falling!" came the shout.

Next came hard shaking, like an earthquake, as Cackle G. landed.

"Hey, everybody!" called Jahdu. He dangled from G.'s mouth as she set him firmly on the ground. "Look who I brought! Come meet my new friend, Cackle G., and hear her story."

Cackle G. was happy. All the little animals came out to meet her. She sat herself gently down so as not to hurt anyone. Jahdu told them of his adventures. "And in the far woods, I saw Prince Charming and Hansel and Little Red . . . and Cackle G. saved the day," Jahdu said, excitedly. He told them all about hip-hopping with the big chicken. Even the giant Trouble leaned around the mountain to hear.

"If you don't come any closer, you can listen," Jahdu told Trouble.

But Trouble was eyeing Cackle G. "You don't by any chance lay golden eggs, do you?" asked the giant.

Cackle G. clucked. She was ready for a fight in case Trouble tried to put a rope around her foot to keep her as a pet.

"Trouble, it was a goose that laid golden eggs, not a chicken!" said Jahdu.

"I'm just a young hen," Cackle G. told him.

"Well, when you grow up, come say hello," said Trouble, and then he turned away, going about his worrisome business.

"Woogily!" said Jahdu. "Where was I?" And he finished the story. All the animals clapped and whistled. They asked to see another hip-hop from Cackle G.

"Maybe you could coast down into the valley," said Raccoon Girl.

"That way, you won't shake us off our mountain," said Wolf Child.

"I won't land here again," said Cackle G., "for I have to get back to the far woods. There, I hope one day all of you will live in my story." She cackled happily. And if chickens smile, she gave Jahdu a big chicken grin.

"Well, never fear, I'll see that your story finds a storybook," Jahdu told her, "and we'll all be there with you in the far woods, too."

"Thank you, Jahdu. You made my month!" said the big chicken. "It's been a lot of fun," she said to everyone. Yes, she did.

"Nice meeting you, Cackle G.," all the animals said.

And then, Cackle G. held out her wings and made a mighty turning around to the left and one huge hip-hop. The big chicken took off from the Mountain of Paths.

"Look out!" said Bear Cub, flattening himself on the ground. There wasn't time to do much else.

"Bye! Oh, bye, Cackle G.," Jahdu called. "I'll see you again some day!"

All the little animals ducked, as the great wings of Cackle G. unfolded.

"Ahhhhh," said the little animals.

There was a rumble, but no earthquake. Then the sky was full of chicken, and of flapping. G.'s wings were like giant curtains ready to catch a skyful of breezes. Next, all grew quiet up there. Everybody stood to watch huge Cackle G. glide out of sight.

"And that's that," said Jahdu.

Everybody said, "What a story!" And, "It's good to see you, Jahdu. Where have you been? We missed you."

They'd forgotten they were very tired of Jahdu. For without a trick-maker around, the Mountain of Paths had become pretty dull.

Jahdu climbed his black gum tree and stretched out among the limbs. Happily, he settled in. It was nice to be home again. He clapped and clapped, because he felt like it. Yes, he did. And he smiled all around, watching this good day become a good night.

JAHDU JOURNEY

J

AHDU came running along at night time. He was headed toward the east. And he was nearly out of his Jahdu dust that had baked into him when he was born.

I hope it will bake into me again, he thought as he ran.

Jahdu was three-and-one-half feet grown. And he had been in the world more than two years. He'd been running everywhere. He'd seen much of the world. He'd learned how to become anyone or anything he wanted to be. Now, he was his own Jahdu self.

"Woogily!" he shouted. "The east surely is far away. When is this long night going to end and let the morning come?"

No answer came from the dark. Jahdu kept running on. He couldn't see anything. He couldn't tell where he'd been or see where he was going.

All at once, he tripped over something. "Wonder what this is lying in the middle of nowhere," he said.

"A-heh, a-heh-heh," a voice spoke, laughing.

"Who in the world is that?" Jahdu asked.

"How you was, Jahdu?" said the voice. "A-heh, a-heh-heh."

Jahdu felt around on the ground. He felt a short tuft of something, like a feathery tail. He felt a pair of webbed feet. Jahdu caught hold of a large, feathered body lying on its back. He touched a queer bird's head with its beak pointing up in the dark. The large bird smelled of fish.

"Phew!" said Jahdu.

"Loon-a-tic," said the bird, "loon-a-tock. Wind my fish, and eat my clock."

"You silly birdy!" Jahdu said. "Why are you lying on the ground?"

It was his old friend Loon. "I'd know you anywhere," Jahdu said, "even in the dark." But never had he come upon Loon on his back.

"How you doing, Jahdu?" Loon asked him.

"Doing just fine," said Jahdu. "Why aren't you flying over Old Ocean searching for your supper?"

"I haven't got the time," Loon said, sadly. "Have you got the time, Jahdu?"

"Now why would I want to go flying over water?" asked Jahdu.

"Have you . . . ," Loon began, in a faraway voice, "got the time?"

"What's the matter with you?" asked Jahdu. "No, I haven't got the time. But it's been the longest night I've ever run through."

"That's what I been thinking," Loon said.

"Here, let me help you up," Jahdu said.

"I staying right, laying low," said Loon. "A-heh, a-heh-heh."

"Well, how long have you been out here?" asked Jahdu.

Loon answered, "A-heh, go ask time; I haven't got the somebody."

"What?" asked Jahdu.

"Just going right, keep on," said crazy Loon. "Light gets until it."

"What in the world!" Jahdu said. He held on to Loon who had started shaking all over.

"*Light way all the not,*" whined Loon. He shouted, "GRAY BUT SOMEWHAT!"

"Oh, Loon, you aren't making any sense," Jahdu said. "Maybe you hit your head when you fell." Gently, he smoothed Loon's long feathers. "You and I are old friends," Jahdu said. "Remember the time I tied your feet together after I put you to sleep? Remember that trick I played?"

"A-heh, yeah," Loon said, calmer now.

"You're not still mad at me, are you, Loon?"

"No, Jahdu. Just find light some me," Loon said.

"Well, come ride with me, then," Jahdu told him. "Climb up and hold on tight."

"You lead the way," he told Loon. "Sniff for water, and there will surely be fish. Then you can eat. I'll eat some fish, too, on my way to the east."

So Jahdu and Loon went running on eastward. That is, Jahdu went running, and Loon went riding and steering. After a long time of darkness, Loon moved his bill to the right of Jahdu.

Jahdu veered to the right and south for what seemed nights. Then, with another nudge from the bill of Loon, he went east again.

After a long time of running, Jahdu said, "I can smell it! Loon, there is salt in the air!"

Jahdu smelled the salt of the sea. Loon was smelling ocean fish. He tried to fly away from Jahdu.

"Stay where you are," Jahdu told him. "We'll be there soon. Look, I can almost see in front of me. It's dark but not quite so black."

Loon groaned. He was dizzy over the smell of fish.

"We're almost there," Jahdu said. "I can hear water lapping at the seashore."

Jahdu stepped over the bank and lost his balance. He and Loon rolled down and — *splash!* — into the chilly water. The sea was full of fish. Loon gobbled them up as fast as he could. Jahdu had a mouthful of water and spat out a parrot fish.

"Woogily!" he said. "What a sudden surprise." He looked all around. "I can almost see things!" he exclaimed.

"Almost," said Loon.

Clinging to each other, Loon and Jahdu climbed up the bank. Loon broke away and tried to get back into the water.

"You've had enough fish," Jahdu said. But Loon only wanted more.

"You are making me angry!" shouted Jahdu. He ran around Loon as fast as he could. Jahdu dust rose out of Jahdu and fell on Loon. But the dust didn't put Loon to sleep as it should have. No, it didn't. For Jahdu's dust was not as strong as it used to be.

"Woogily!" said Jahdu. He ran around Loon a second time. This time Loon fell fast asleep.

I still have some magic, thought Jahdu, but I'd better get to the east before it's all gone. He rested awhile, then he woke Loon to say good-bye.

"Leave me here in the dark — don't," Loon said. He sounded ready to cry. "Put me sleep again — want to? But don't leave me 'wake."

"I have to go," Jahdu said. "You saw how weak my magic dust is. I have to get to the east and get new dust."

"Take along me," Loon said mournfully.

"I can't carry you all that way, Loon. I'm sorry," said Jahdu.

"But it dark!" Loon cried. "I lost. I scared."

"Yes, it's a long kind of dark," Jahdu said. "Do you remember when it started?"

"No," Loon said. "I only afraid. I all-time thinking of scared and hungry."

"Well, just for you, I'm going to find out what happened to the light."

"For me?" asked Loon.

"You're my friend, aren't you?" said Jahdu.

"And will be ever, Jahdu," said Loon.

"Then it's settled," Jahdu told him. "You stay right here where you have as much fish as you want. So good-bye, friend Loon," Jahdu said. Already, Jahdu was running away. "I'll see you again after I've visited the east."

"Good-bye, a-heh, Jahdu," Loon called sadly.

Jahdu went running on. He had what was left of his magic back within him. He was alone again in darkness. The darkness did have shadow now. Jahdu followed the shadow dark toward the east.

"Woogily! I'm glad to be running along again," said Jahdu. "I'm going home to be reborn!"

How Jahdu Found What He Wished He Hadn't

JAHDU went running through darkness with Shadow just ahead of him. It was a while before he knew that the shadow was his. It was running, too.

How is it my shadow is here when there is little light? Jahdu wondered. How did it get away from me again? Oh, because my power is weak.

Shadow stopped its running. When Jahdu caught up with it, it started running alongside Jahdu.

"How you doing, Jahdu?" Shadow asked.

"I'm doing all right," Jahdu told him. "I see you are up to your old tricks. When I have my magic back, you won't get away from me."

"Oh, but you see," said Shadow, "I'm not just *your* shadow in this dark time. I'm everybody's shadow as long as there is no light."

"How long hasn't there been light?" Jahdu asked.

"All I know is that times have changed," said Shadow. "I think there won't be much light anymore. It is going to stay dark forever."

"Oh, no, I don't believe that," said Jahdu.

"Didn't I just tell you?" said Shadow. "I'm part of you, so I must be telling the truth."

"It's true, you are part of me," Jahdu said, "but as you say, so is everybody a part of you, too. I don't think it will be dark forever."

"No?" said Shadow.

"No," said Jahdu.

"All right, then," said Shadow, and he was gone.

Jahdu was plunged into darkness with no Shadow anywhere.

"How do you like that?" called Shadow.

"You'll never amount to anything!" shouted Jahdu.

"Maybe not," called back Shadow, "but you're the one out there with nobody to guide you."

"I don't need you or anybody to guide me!" Jahdu yelled.

"No?" said Shadow. "Then why are you heading west?"

Jahdu stopped dead in his tracks. Woogily! he thought. I let Shadow trick me.

"Hey!" Jahdu called out. "That was a good trick. How about heading me toward the east again."

"Sorry, Jahdu, you are on your own," said Shadow from far away, "and before you reach the east, you are in for a shock."

Sweetly, Jahdu called, "Shadow? Oh, Shadow?" But Shadow would not answer him.

Jahdu hurried on, and he had no idea which way he went. He ran for nights and nights. Sometimes, he stumbled over small animals. And once he tripped over a farmer.

"I haven't got a minute to waste," said the farmer. Yet he made no move to go. He lay there in the dark as if he had all the time in the world.

Jahdu left the farmer behind, or ahead—he couldn't tell which in all that dark.

One night the earth trembled; the darkness throbbed in huge, moving spaces.

"Ga-roammm, ga-roammm," came a sound. "GA-ROAMMM, GA-ROAMMM."

Jahdu stopped still in the dark. "Who is it, please?" he called, in a trembly voice.

"Mammoths, us—how you doing, stranger?" said so many voices from on high. It was a herd of great woolly mammoths moving across the earth.

"Wait!" Jahdu called. "You lived a long time ago. Wait for me! Are you heading east? Wait for me!"

"Ga-roammm, can't stop, little stranger, we haven't got the time," called the mammoths from a long way off.

"Just tell me if you are heading east!" Jahdu yelled.

"Ga-roam-roammmmm," came the mammoths' reply. Then the earth settled down again, and they were gone.

Why are mammoths here when they lived so long ago? Jahdu wondered. He ran and ran, thinking that mammoths lived at the beginning of time.

The first sun rose. The first light came, thought Jahdu. Mammoths lived . . . and time began! So, I must be close to the east. And the closer I come to it, the further back in time I go.

Jahdu thought he was heading east. Not long and he was seeing something clearer through the darkness.

"Woogily!" said Jahdu. The darkness up ahead was piled up like mountains.

Jahdu climbed as fast as he could. By the time he reached the top of a foothill, he had discovered a whole mountain range.

"Woogily!" he said. "There are more than fifty-two mountains that I can see."

The mountains lay deep in shadow.

"Oh, my goodness!" said Jahdu. He started to run down the foothill. For the mountains began to heave and shake in rhythm with the shadow that rose and fell.

"I wish they wouldn't," Jahdu said.

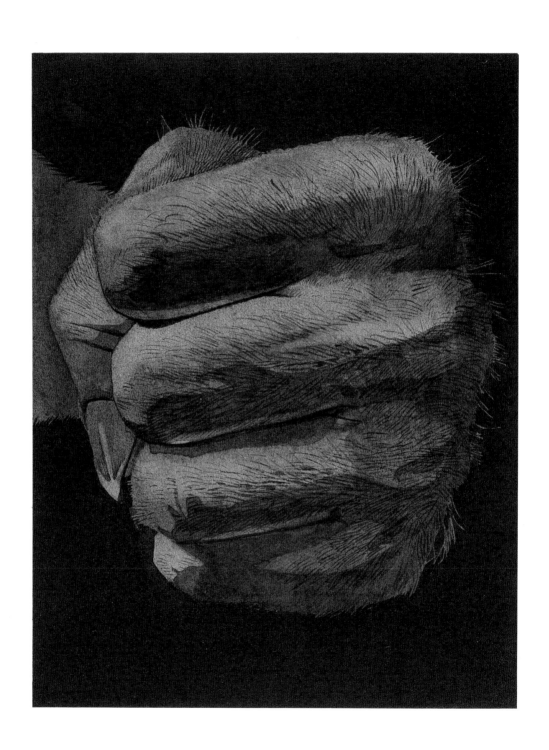

Before Jahdu knew it, the giant Trouble had him cupped in his strong left hand.

"I wish you didn't," Jahdu groaned to the giant.

But he was caught, and there wasn't a thing he could do about that.

No, he couldn't.

Jahdu Lights the Way

H OW you doing, Trouble?" asked Jahdu, kindly. He still fit snugly in Trouble's fist. "I never thought I'd run into you out here in the dark."

"I said you were in for a B I G shock," called Shadow, who lay on one side of the giant.

"How are you, little friend? And who might you be, running along out here all by your lonesome?" Trouble asked Jahdu. He sat him gently down.

"Don't you remember me? I'm Jahdu who is always running along," said Jahdu.

"I'm sure I don't know you at all," said Trouble. "I haven't ever come across anyone called Jahdu."

"Well, I came across you more than once some time ago."

"There's no time ago that I know of," said Trouble. "There is only here and now."

"Well for goodness sake!" said Jahdu. "But tell me, do you still have your earring with a barrel hanging from it? A barrel as big as a standpipe?"

Trouble was silent.

"Look there," said Shadow to Jahdu. "You can just make out the shape of a big barrel in the dark."

Sure enough, Jahdu could see the barrel in the dimness, on its side.

"Trouble, don't you want to put me in that barrel over there?" asked Jahdu.

"Not unless you want me to," Trouble said.

"Oh, no, I don't want you to," Jahdu told him. "But maybe you know where the east is — do you? It's a direction," Jahdu prompted the giant.

"Well then, that might be the east behind my shoulder," said Trouble.

"Would you lift me up so I can see over there?" asked Jahdu.

"Take a good look," Trouble said. And he let Jahdu see.

At the far edge of darkness, way faraway behind Trouble's shoulder, Jahdu saw a pale color.

"Woogily!" he hollered. Yes, he did. "There it is! Way out there is the east, the place I've been looking for. And way out there is something dim. Trouble, it's the only pale color I've seen in all of this darkness."

"There *is* color over there," agreed Trouble, looking over his shoulder. "It is the only color I know of."

"Once there was plenty of light," said Jahdu. "And once there was plenty of time. But now something holds the light in the east. And it keeps back time. That's why we have so little of both."

"Don't know what you are talking about, little Jahdu," Trouble said.

"Oh well, never mind. You can set me down now," Jahdu said, and Trouble did.

"Do you have a match?" Jahdu asked him. "I'd like to see my way to the east."

Trouble was silent. But Shadow spoke up. "Look in your shirt pocket," Shadow said to the giant.

"Oh, you mean these," Trouble said, patting his pocket. "I forgot I had them."

"Could you lend me one?" asked Jahdu.

"Sure," Trouble said. "I've got plenty."

"And would you light it for me, too? Just whisk it along your pant leg very fast," said Jahdu.

"All right," said Trouble. He brought out a match the size of a sapling. He whisked it along his trousers. There was a burst of yellow light.

"Woogily!" shouted Jahdu.

"Hardly light enough to see by," said Trouble.

"It looks like a great light to me," said Jahdu.

Trouble has forgotten most things, Jahdu thought. I guess the closer you come to the east, the less you remember. Something is keeping back time and light. And that holds back Trouble's memory from him.

"Trouble, would you put that barrel over near the east?" Jahdu asked the giant.

"I don't mind," Trouble said. He didn't even ask why.

"And would you light it with another match?"

"I don't mind," Trouble said again. He picked up the empty barrel and flicked it over his right shoulder. It landed in darkness near the east.

"And would you set me down in the darkness, about a half mile from the barrel?"

"If that's what you want," said Trouble. He did as Jahdu asked.

"NOW, GIANT TROUBLE," Jahdu shouted as loud as he could, "LIGHT THE BARREL."

Trouble chuckled a sound like a waterfall. "All right," he said.

There was a burst of burning light like a forest on fire. Through the fiery night, Jahdu ran to the east as fast as he could. Behind him, he could hear the shadow sighing. Jahdu looked back. Shadow had been swallowed up by the firelight.

Jahdu could see Trouble. Yes, he could. The burning barrel made a great light. Yes, it did. Trouble could see Jahdu, and Trouble could remember for as long as the firelight lasted.

The earth shook as Trouble stood to his giant height.

His face was rain-cloud dark and full of stormy anger. His feet looked as big as ocean ships; his legs as long as highways.

The great right hand of Trouble swooped down and just missed Jahdu running hard.

"Woogily!" Jahdu cried, looking back. Trouble's left hand was packed full of donkeys and birds and even some people. They had wandered in the dark and had got caught by Trouble in the firelight.

"Jahdu!" Trouble roared in a voice like a hurricane.

Jahdu ran on and on.

He heard Trouble say, "My barrel. You made me burn it. Now where will I keep my friends?"

"You have to let them go," Jahdu called. He didn't care if Trouble heard him or not. "I outsmarted you again, you big old Trouble. You'll have to let your *friends* run along like me!"

As the burning barrel light began to fade, Trouble lost his memory again. He was surprised to find monkeys and babies clutched in his fist. He set them gently down in the growing shadow. The light of the barrel flickered and went out. Trouble lay flat on his back on the ground, looking as long and as dark as a whole mountain range.

That is how Jahdu found his way to the east and how he took care of Trouble for the third time.

JAHDU found his old oven in a grove of trees. The oven door creaked as he opened it. He lay down on the rusted oven rack to be reborn.

"Woogily! Jahdu is almost too long for this oven," he said, softly.

The oven door squeaked closed. Dusty heat as hot as the sun swirled around Jahdu. The heat baked deep into him. And the dust settled on him and down in him like sauce on a sparerib.

Ah, that's good, he thought. I will have magic Jahdu dust to last me a long, long time.

Jahdu baked smooth and tender. As he baked, he grew as a boy of the east would grow, all bundled in fur. He wore fur leggings and snowshoes. Then he slept for a peaceful silence of heat and rest.

When he awoke he felt calm and new. He stretched his young boy's arms. He yawned and climbed out of his old oven. Then he bowed deeply to the oven, for now he admired all things that were old. Bowing, he backed out of the grove of trees.

Jahdu tramped quickly through a wasteland in the east. Westward, he again saw the darkness he had gone through to get there.

"Woogily!" he said and jumped high over a snowbank. His snowshoes were soon caked with snow.

"I'm glad to be a boy with yellow skin and black, black hair," he said. "But this east is a cold and frozen place."

He had a bow and arrows slung over his shoulder. Fruits and nuts were in a bundle tied to his waist and would be his supper.

Smiling, Jahdu touched his bow. I'm a bold hunter of the east, he thought. I've been reborn as well. I can help Loon and everybody. And I'll find out what happened to the light.

As Jahdu ran, he found only shade covering all the snow and ice. The sun seemed far from the earth. And he could find no light anywhere.

"Everything is gray," Jahdu said out loud. "Wonder why the sun is so weak."

"It's the way I like it," said a voice. "I am content in all of my days."

Jahdu stopped in his tracks. Fear moved up and down his spine.

"Hallooo," Jahdu said, looking all around.

"How are you doing, Jahdu?" said the voice.

"I'm doing fine," he said, "but how do you know me? Who are you, and *where* are you?"

"I'm Yin, who knows all," said the voice. "I am the shade all around you."

"Ah," said Jahdu, "you are the shade on the top of things and at the side of things. Are you my shadow, too?"

"I'm Yin," said Yin. "I am colored the palest green and gray and white."

"Then you are the pale color I saw as I came through the dark," said Jahdu.

"I am," said Yin.

"And you must be the keeper of this long, gray time," said Jahdu.

"I do have my way here," said Yin. "But there is another over there on the boulder."

Jahdu went near the boulder at the edge of the shade field. He hadn't noticed it in a patch of shadeless snow.

"How are you, Jahdu?" the boulder seemed to say.

"I'm doing all right," said Jahdu, shielding his eyes. The boulder blinded him, it was so bright. "I never talked to a boulder before," Jahdu said.

"You never will," said the voice. "Boulders decided a long time ago not to talk."

"Then who is speaking to me, please?" asked Jahdu.

"I am Yang," said the voice. "I am the only warmth and light in all of this land."

"Ah," Jahdu said. "I've hunted all over for you! I have friends who need you. There is darkness everywhere in the world, and everybody is afraid."

"Darkness is the shade of Yin, and Yin is strong here," said Yang. "Thunder is Yin's friend who holds the clouds together. I may light only this boulder."

Thunder rolled overhead with a boom that shook the ground.

"What an awful noise!" said Jahdu.

"I don't care for Thunder at all," said Yang.

"Neither do I," Jahdu said. "I don't like the cold, either. Could I sit on the boulder and warm myself in your light? My legs are freezing."

"I don't mind if you do," said Yang.

Jahdu climbed upon the boulder. The light spread all over him and on down the rock. Ice began to melt at the base of the boulder, and snow around it vanished.

"Watch out, Yang!" Yin, the shade, called out. "You come too near my field."

Yang moved to the very top, around Jahdu, where he glowed with anger.

"Don't be angry with the light," Jahdu said to Yin. "It was trying to warm my legs."

"I say take care," Yin said.

Jahdu had to pull his legs up to keep them in the light and warmth.

"Everything is changed," Yang said, softly so Yin wouldn't hear. "Yin chooses where to be, and I have no choice."

"Yin does seem powerful," said Jahdu. "And you are barely able to cover me from head to toe."

"It's not fair," Yang said.

"Woogily!" said Jahdu. He had an idea. "I'm going to have me some fun!" He leaped out into the snow and the shade of Yin.

Jahdu made tracks all over the shade.

"Stop it, Jahdu," said Yin. "Get back on the boulder where you belong."

Thunder boomed above Jahdu.

Jahdu started stamping around in his snowshoes faster and faster. Strong Jahdu dust rose out of him and fell on the shade of Yin. Softly, Yin sighed, for Jahdu dust had put her to sleep.

"Yang, look at this!" Jahdu said. "I put Yin to sleep. Come down and see for yourself."

Carefully, Yang let his light spread down the boulder. Then Yang stopped to listen. Yin snored gently as Thunder boomed above.

Ice and snow melted. Pale light was everywhere in the field that had been Yin.

Jahdu jumped and leaped happily in the light.

"Ho!" said Yang. "I am large!"

Suddenly, Jahdu and Yang saw something on the north edge of the field of snow. Something was huge and slow, and it was coming. Yang slid back to his boulder. He held himself on the very top.

Yin woke up with a start. In the east, Jahdu could put things to sleep, but there was power in the land that was stronger than his magic.

"What is it that's coming?" Jahdu asked.

"It's Yin's goddess," whispered Yang.

"But who is she?" asked Jahdu.

"She's nothing small," said Yang.

The Goddess of Yin was the largest turtle in the world.

Diamond shapes the size of double doors were patterned on her shell. In the center of each diamond were long and short line markings. The turtle's feet were as wide as rooms, and wrinkles of age hung like curtains from her long, rising neck.

"Woogily!" whispered Jahdu. "The Goddess of Yin is a great turtle. Where in the world is she going?"

"She goes home," said Yang. "She lives in the lake to the south. Mists of winter hang there like a shroud."

"I see," said Jahdu, staring off at the lake. "Look how she pulls all of the snow and ice of winter along with her. But look again! Behind her, everything is turning green. It's getting warm!"

"So it seems," said Yang, sadly.

"Once the turtle is in her lake, I bet summer will come. And then there will be light everywhere," said Jahdu.

"Wait and see," said Yang, more sadly than ever.

Old Yang doesn't know how to have a good time, thought Jahdu. Everything was about to be all right. Winter was going to be over, and darkness, too.

The shade of Yin flowed around the turtle for as long as it took her to reach her water home. Then the turtle sank beneath the waters. The mists of winter parted from around the lake. Trees and flowers grew everywhere. Thunder sounded distantly, and grass grew thick and long.

"I'm getting hot," said Jahdu. He stood in the full light of Yang, which was everywhere. He pulled off most of his fur wrappings.

"Be sure to keep your clothes on top of my boulder," Yang told him.

"I don't need them," Jahdu said.

"Do as I tell you!"

Jahdu didn't like Yang ordering him about. But he did as he was told. He found his snowshoes and placed them beneath his clothes.

"Dig under the boulder," Yang told him. "Place your food in the hole. You will need it when winter comes again."

"But winter is over," Jahdu said.

"It will come again! Do as I say," said Yang.

Yang's getting cranky, Jahdu thought. I'd better do as he says.

So Jahdu buried his food bundle beneath the boulder. Then he lay down fully in the light and got himself a deep golden tan. When he grew hot, he found a tree to lie under. Now, the sound of Thunder was far off. Jahdu, boy of the east, smiled and closed his eyes.

Jahdu Sees the True Light

HOW hot it has become," Jahdu said. "I'm glad to rest in this shade." The shade cooled him, and he felt peaceful. "Yin, is that you?" he asked.

"I am here," said Yin, who was shade. She laughed a soft sound.

Thunder came nearer, and Jahdu opened his eyes. Out of the heat and light of the wasteland streaked a red bird. Like a stream of fire, the red bird landed. It walked toward Jahdu.

Jahdu laughed. "Come to me, pretty bird. Let me touch your feathers." The red bird had a long tail that flamed in the light of Yang. Wherever the bird walked, bush and grasses burned with fire.

"It's summer now," said Yang. "But be careful, Jahdu. Don't touch the bird, it's hot!"

The red bird came close to Jahdu. Jahdu reached out to stroke his gleaming tail. "Woogily!" he said, "I can feel your heat. I like you, Firebird."

"How you doing, Jahdu?" asked the red bird. It walked along past Jahdu. There was a clap of Thunder quite near. The red bird flapped its wings in a flash of color and flew away.

"Is it going to rain?" asked Jahdu. But Yin was silent.

"There's Thunder, but there are no clouds," Jahdu said. "I am cool. Where has all the heat gone?"

Clouds massed above him and over the wasteland as far as the edge of darkness. The clouds closed out the light.

"Ah," sighed Yin, softly. "I am cool. I am large."

A tiger roared on the far side of the great she-turtle's water world.

Jahdu got to his knees in a crouch. "A tiger, here?" he said. He fitted an arrow to his bow.

"Summer has passed," Yin said. "It's autumn, and the white tiger comes to eat whatever there is to eat in this land."

"A hunter tiger!" said Jahdu. "I could use his fur in winter and the tiger meat for food."

"Hurry to me, Jahdu!" cried Yang.

Jahdu ran for the boulder. He pulled on his fur clothing. The air had turned cold. He crept near the lake.

Jahdu stalked Tiger, and Tiger stalked Jahdu. Thunder rolled right above Tiger's head. Tiger paused, as Yin and Yang changed shade to light and light to shade. Tiger's eyes could not see so well.

After a long time of stalking, Jahdu lowered his bow and arrow. "Even with your help, I can't catch Tiger," Jahdu said to Yin and Yang, "and even though Tiger is swift and cunning, he can't catch me."

"It is true," said Yang.

"It is the way things are here," said Yin. "Tiger must come here, and Tiger must leave again. You cannot kill him."

Jahdu walked slowly back to the boulder.

"So then, you do have time here in the east," Jahdu said to Yang.

"There are seasons," Yang said. "There is time for me, but not enough."

Snow fell as Thunder sounded. Ice formed on the lake of the great turtle. The white tiger left the wasteland. Plants and trees quickly died. Yang was careful to cover all of Jahdu with light so that the winter would not harm him.

"How can there be just time enough for only one day of summer and autumn?" Jahdu asked.

"There has been only one day of warmth and light since the Great Change," said Yang.

"The Great Change?" asked Jahdu. "Tell me about it."

"Long ago, the turtle belonged the same to both Yin and me," said Yang. "I had all of the light of the sun, and Yin kept the darkness of the moon. The turtle brought my summer in its season and Yin's winter in its time."

"Then what happened?" asked Jahdu.

Before Yang could answer, water broke out of the icy surface of the lake. The great turtle struggled out of the black water. Ever so slowly, she came, pulling shadow and cold of winter. Where she passed, the landscape filled with ice and snow.

"What happened is this," said Yang. "Our turtle has grown old. She cannot travel as quickly as she once did. There was a time when she rested in her water world. Then there would be summer. But now, she enters her lake, but rises quickly out of it before her great feet grow stiff. Always she moves, like a sleepless old aunt, unable to stay still."

"Ah," said Jahdu, "the great turtle is ancient." He bowed deeply with respect.

"Winter has settled in," said Yang.

"It's a grim winter, too," said Jahdu. "Do you think the turtle will die in one of these winters?"

"I think the turtle will live an old one forever," said Yang.

"And how long is forever?" asked Jahdu.

"It is as long as traveling in a circle," said Yang.

"Circles have no end," said Jahdu. He bowed to the great turtle again.

"Nothing is fair in this life," said Yang. "The turtle should be my Goddess as she used to be."

Jahdu plucked lightly on his bowstring, making a sweet sound. Laughter played about his mouth. He didn't say a word. Jahdu thought and thought. When he came to the end of his thinking, he had thought of a plan.

"Watch this," Jahdu said to Yang. He fitted an arrow to his bow. He crept up behind the turtle, who had not gone far. Jahdu bowed deeply to the turtle, then took careful aim. He pulled back on the arrow and string. He let them loose at the same time.

"Whang!" went the bowstring as the arrow streaked across the wasteland.

"Ka-whuck-it!" went the arrow as it hit the turtle through the middle of her tail.

"Ker-purtle!" said Jahdu. "I've got me a turtle."

The Goddess of Yin spun around in a slow circle. She took a deep breath, sucking in a snowfield. She blew out a roar that knocked Thunder into pieces all over the sky. It broke Yang's boulder into pebbles and lifted Jahdu off his feet in a blizzard.

Jahdu flew through the air in the worst snowstorm he'd ever seen. He grabbed hold of the last tree still left standing.

"Woogily!" he said. "This is some turtlestorm!" Through the blizzard,

Jahdu could see the Goddess of Yin turning around and around trying to get the arrow loose from her tail. Her huge feet stamping around made a gigantic pit in the wasteland of winter. Down and down went the she-turtle in the pit. Finally, she caught hold of the arrow and tore it loose. By then, Jahdu's plan had worked.

"Yang!" shouted Jahdu. "Where are you, Yang?"

"Here," said Yang, in the tiniest voice.

Jahdu looked down and all around. At last he found Yang. Yang was in a snowflake. The flake glowed like the sun on Jahdu's fur coat.

"I am small," cried Yang, in the tiniest voice. "My boulder is gone — help me!"

"The turtle has made a crater," said Jahdu. "And the turtle's roar has torn Thunder into bits and pieces!"

Sure enough, Thunder could make a noise like drums rolling. But it couldn't boom anymore, like the sky falling.

"There are trees growing," said Jahdu, "and plants and grass!"

"I am comfortable!" cried Yang, for suddenly he was everywhere. "I am large!"

For six months, the turtle struggled to get out of her pit. While she labored, the wasteland bloomed with wild flowers, and the sun shone brightly. But finally, one hot summer day, the great turtle worked herself free. When her massive head looked over the edge of the pit, the weather changed to the coolness of fall.

"Now there will be time enough," Yang said to Jahdu.

"Yes, because the turtle will have a hard time climbing out of her pit," Jahdu said.

"And when she's free, she'll be unable to change her ways," said Yang. She'll go north pulling winter along."

"And when she comes back?" asked Jahdu, leaping into the air.

"She'll fall back into the pit!" cried Yang.

"Woogily!" said Jahdu. "Summer will last a long time while she struggles free."

Yin sighed. "My Goddess will never reach her water world," she said.

"But that's good!" said Yang. "She is now a land turtle, and her old feet won't grow stiff anymore."

Then Yang told Jahdu, "The great Goddess once again belongs to both Yin and me. The world is as it was and should be."

"Never again will Thunder be strong enough to hold the clouds together," Jahdu said. "The red bird will have time to prance and preen. And the white tiger can stalk a long while."

"Thank you, Jahdu," said Yang.

"Glad to be of help," said Jahdu.

Yin stayed quiet, no doubt thinking dark thoughts.

"Come back whenever you can," Yang said, kindly.

"I'll do that," said Jahdu.

Yin said nothing at all.

Then Jahdu went running along. There was light all around the world. Darkness came only with the setting sun. There were people in the light, each person with its shadow. There was a giant, Trouble, searching for a new barrel. There was a crazy Loon who was no longer afraid, at least not in the daytime.

"All's right with the world," said Jahdu. And then, "Word off! Jahdu is jumping off this boy of the east. Jahdu is not a boy of the east anymore!"

All at once, he was his own Jahdu self again. Yes, he was.

"I'm a trickmaker!" he shouted. "Word on! I am the one and only Jahdu."

AND SO HE IS, UNTIL THIS GO

OD DAY BECOMES TOMORROW.

AFTERWORD

YEARS AGO, I created the character called Jahdu (no last name) who is always running along. Jahdu is a folkloric, small creature, somehow mythical, born in an ancient oven beside two loaves of baking bread — the Jahdu creation story! One loaf of bread baked brown, and the other baked black. But Jahdu didn't bake at all. Yet, ever after, black and brown have been Jahdu's favorite colors. And the old oven gives him his own special magic.

I wrote two collections of Jahdu stories and one picture-book Jahdu — *The Time-Ago Tales of Jahdu* (1969); *More Tales of Jahdu* (1973); and *Jahdu* (Read-Alone, 1980). I am fortunate to now have the chance to remodel all of these stories for the children of the 1990s and the twenty-first century in *The All Jahdu Storybook*. *The All Jahdu Storybook* also includes four new tales: "Jahdu in a Little Bit of Trouble," "How Jahdu Lost His Voice," "Jahdu in the Far Woods," and "Jahdu Meets the Big Chicken."

In the original stories, a character, Mama Luka, takes care of the child, Lee Edward, while his parents work. She tells Jahdu stories to entertain him, picking a story out of the air and tasting it before each telling.

The reader views Jahdu through Mama Luka's eyes as she tells Jahdu tales to Lee Edward.

In this way, the stories were introduced through a frame — Mama Luka telling the tales as Lee Edward listened and asked questions. The reader saw Jahdu as if looking at a picture or watching through a window. And even though writing about Mama Luka was always a pleasure, the character now seems to be an obstacle to the reader's enjoyment of Jahdu. I believe this is because influences in the youth culture twenty years ago were different from those of today. The original stories were quite popular in their time; and yet I think it's true that today's young people want to get closer to their heroes.

The All Jahdu Storybook allows them to do that by presenting the original stories as well as the new ones without the Mama Luka frame. Now readers can feel they are right up front and running along with Jahdu, without any separation from him.

These remodeled stories introduce characters that express the timelessness of folklore and folk history. And yet they hinge on no specific traditions. Jahdu is still the all-out trickster, magical and devilish, good and bad, imp and elf. He is the age-old transformer, the shapeshifter at liberty to become anything or anyone.

Think of Jahdu as representing me, the author, having fun and playing tricks. Jahdu stories came directly from my attempt to do in words what members of my storytelling family did aloud: to make up and *give* a tale.

The difference is that I have written my stories down. Still, I can read them aloud. And I often do, keeping in mind the fine tale-tellers of my own family. I hope the reader will feel free to try them aloud, as well.

— Virginia Hamilton

The pictures in this book were painted with
transparent watercolors on paper handmade for the
Royal Watercolor Society in 1982 by J. Barcham Green.
Lettering is by Reassurance Wunder based on forms
originally drawn by Rudolph Koch.
The text type was set in Sabon by Thompson Type, San Diego, California.
Color separations were made by Bright Arts, Ltd., Singapore.
Printed by Holyoke Lithograph, Springfield, Massachusetts
Bound by The Book Press, Inc., Brattleboro, Vermont
Production supervision by Warren Wallerstein and Ginger Boyer
Designed by Barry Moser